Aman Chiu 著

圖像速學英語介詞
Learn prepositions in English
through pictures

U0132427

商務印書館

圖像速學英語介詞

Learn prepositions in English through pictures

作　　者：Aman Chiu

責任編輯：黃家麗

出　　版：商務印書館 (香港) 有限公司

　　　　　香港筲箕灣耀興道 3 號東滙廣場 8 樓

　　　　　http://www.commercialpress.com.hk

發　　行：香港聯合書刊物流有限公司

　　　　　香港新界大埔汀麗路 36 號中華商務印刷大廈 3 字樓

印　　刷：美雅印刷製本有限公司

　　　　　九龍官塘榮業街 6 號海濱工業大廈 4 樓 A 室

版　　次：2015 年 5 月第 1 版第 1 次印刷

　　　　　© 2015 商務印書館 (香港) 有限公司

　　　　　ISBN 978 962 07 1900 4

　　　　　Printed in Hong Kong

目錄
CONTENTS

Section 1: The Basics of Prepositions

 介詞基本知識

何謂介詞？

介詞又叫前置詞，用來表示詞與詞之間的聯結方式。它是一種虛詞，通常後接名詞或代詞，不需要重讀，在句中不單獨用作任何句子成份，只表示其後的名詞（或相當於名詞的詞語）與其他句子成份的關係。

介詞種類

介詞從字形上區分，有以下兩類：

1) 簡單介詞，即只由一個單詞構成，例如：

at	in	inside	into	of
by	about	for	from	except
since	near	with	without	upon

2) 短語介詞，即由兩個或兩個以上的單詞組合構成，例如：

because of	by means of	out of
instead of	in front of	on behalf of
in spite of		

按詞義分類一般包括以下五種：

1) 時間介詞，最常見的例子包括 in (in January, in the morning)、on (on Sunday, on my birthday) 和 at (at 10 o'clock, at lunch time)。

2) 地點介詞，最常見的例子也是 in (in a car, in the library)、on (on the wall, on a table) 和 at (at the bus stop, at the entrance)。

3) 方向介詞，最常見的例子包括 to (go to school)、through (drive through a tunnel) 和 into (jump into the pool)。

4) 表示施行者的介詞，例如 by (by Shakespeare)。

5) 表示工具的介詞，例如 by (by car) 和 with (with a hammer)

其他介詞種類，還可以表示比較、對立、讓步、組成部份、計算、原因及方式等。

英語詞彙數以萬計，相比之下，介詞佔的比例很小，只有 100 多個，但可以說是最活躍詞類，它們使用範圍之廣，使用頻率之高及難度之大，恐怕也是其他詞類比不上的，所以中國人用英語進行書面或口頭表達時，往往出現遺漏介詞或誤用介詞的錯誤，因此各類考試語法的結構部份均有這方面的測試內容。

能夠好好掌握介詞用法，確實是學好英語的關鍵所在。本書精要地闡釋各種介詞和介詞短語的意義和用法，輔以圖像和大量例句，務求透過簡明實用的例子，讓讀者更懂得如何運用介詞。一些容易混淆或用錯的介詞更會附加註解，說明它們在語法上的正確用法和注意事項，幫助讀者加強運用介詞的能力。

01 PREPOSITIONS FOR TIME 時間介詞

介詞表示詞與詞之間的關係，例如時間關係，可分以下六類。

1.1 at, on, in

at、on、in 都可表示時間，但因用法不同，會使許多學生產生混淆。但只要記住 at 代表「一時一刻、非常短促」的時間，on 代表「一天」，而 in 則代表「一段頗長」的時間，便可以把它們掌握得更好。

 ### 1.1.1 怎樣用
Usage

用途

at 用於特定時刻。

HOURS

 例
- at 3 pm
- at ten o'clock
- at breakfast
- at sunset
- at night

甚麼是特定時刻？一點鐘、兩點鐘是特定時刻，午餐、晚餐、日出、日落也是特定時刻。at present / at the moment / at the same time 都是特定時刻，但以下情況則屬例外，用 in 不用 at：

- in the morning / in the afternoon / in the evening

用途

on 用於日期和特定日子。

DAYS

 例
- on January the first
- on Tuesday
- on my birthday
- on sports day
- on Christmas Eve

日期指特定的年、月、日或一週裏的某天；特定日子包括一年裏不同的節慶、假期。但以下情況除外，用 at 不用 on：

- at the weekend / at Easter / at Christmas

用途

in 用於星期、月份、年份、世紀或更長的時間。

WEEKS, MONTHS, YEARS, ETC.

 例
- in two weeks
- in June
- in the winter
- in 2013
- in the 90s
- in the next century

1.1.2 注意
Notes

⊗ 以下情況無需用 at、on、in。

1) 在 last 和 next 之前不用，

- I'll see you next Monday. 我下星期一見你。
  (not on next Monday)
- I went to Taipei last June. 我去年六月去了台北。
  (not in last June)

2) 在 every 前不用，

- They go to Japan every Easter. 他們每年復活節都去日本。
  (not at every Easter)

3) 在 this 和 that 前不用，

- We'll call you this evening. 我們今晚會打電話給你。
  (not in this evening)

4) 在 yesterday 和 tomorrow 等前不用，

- I ran into John yesterday. 我昨天偶然遇上約翰。
  (not on yesterday)
- See you tomorrow. 明天見。(not on tomorrow)
- I last saw him the day before yesterday. 我前天最後一次見到他。
  (not on the day before yesterday)
- School starts two days after tomorrow. 學校大後天開課。
  (not on two days after tomorrow)

5) at、on、in 也是位置介詞，另參見 2.1。

1.1.3 用法速查表
Speed check

at hours 特定時刻	on days 日期或特定日子	in weeks, months, years, decades, centuries 星期、月份、年份、 世紀或更長時間
at 3 o' clock	on Sunday	in August
at 10.30 am	on Wednesdays	in summer
at noon	on 5 July	in 1997
at dinner time	on 25 December, 2016	in the 1990s
at bedtime	on Christmas Day	in the next century
at sunrise	on New Year's Eve	in the Ice Age*
at sunset	on Dragon Boat Festival**	in the past
at the moment	on my birthday	in the future
以下慣用短語屬於例外		
at the weekend	on Tuesday morning	in the morning
at weekends	on Saturday mornings	in the mornings
at Christmas	on Sunday afternoons	in the afternoon(s)
at Easter	on Monday evening	in the evening

*Ice Age: 冰川期；冰河時代
**Dragon Boat Festival: 端午節

1.2 past, to

past 和 to 用於報時，比如回答 What's the time now? 或 What time is it? 的問題，兩者在用法上的區別可見以下口訣：1 to 30 PAST, over 30 TO（一到 30 分鐘用 past；超過 30 分鐘用 to）。

⚡ 1.2.1 怎樣用
Usage

用途

past　用於正點前，以 30 分鐘之內的時間為限，說明幾點過了多少分鐘。

例
- five past five 5 時 5 分
- ten past eight 8 時 10 分
- twenty-two past five 5 時 22 分

past 除了可用於數詞之後，還可用於名詞詞組 a quarter（一刻鐘，即 15 分鐘）之後。

例
- It was a quarter past five. 時間是 5 點 15 分。

past 也可用於代詞 half 之後。

例
- It was half past eight. 時間是 8 點半。

用途

to　用於正點前，以 30 分鐘以內的時間為限，說明尚餘多少分鐘才到達某個正點。

例
- twenty-one to five 4 時 39 分
- ten to nine 8 時 50 分
- five to eight 7 時 55 分

to 除了可用於數詞之後，還可用於名詞詞組 a quarter（一刻鐘，即 15 分鐘）之後。

 • It was a quarter to five. 時間是 4 點 45 分。

⊕ **比較中英文**

to 用於分針過了 6 但未到 12 的時間，變相是要倒數，但要用下一個小時，例如「6 時 35 分」會說成 twenty-five to seven（切忌說成 twenty-five to six）。

 ## 1.2.2 注意
Notes

1) to 不能用於代詞 half 之後，沒有 It was half to eight. 這個說法。

2) 報時也可直說小時及分鐘，不受 past 或 to 的限制，例：

• 9 07　　nine oh seven (= seven past nine)
　　　　　九時零七分
• 9 15　　nine fifteen (= a quarter past nine)
　　　　　九時十五分；九時一刻
• 9 23　　nine twenty-three (= twenty-three past nine)
　　　　　九時二十三分
• 9 30　　nine thirty (= half past nine)
　　　　　九時三十分；九時半
• 9 45　　nine forty-five (= a quarter to ten)
　　　　　九時四十五分；九時三刻
• 9 55　　nine fifty-five (= five to ten)
　　　　　九時五十五分

1.2.3 用法速查表
Speed check

past = (of time) after 幾點過了多少分鐘	to = (of time) before 尚餘多少分鐘才到幾點
ten past eight 八時十分	ten to eight 七時五十分
twenty past five 五時二十分	twenty to five 四時四十分
a quarter past five 五時十五分	a quarter to five 四點四十五分
half past eight 八時半 *	

* 沒有half to eight的說法

1.3 after, before, by, in

作為時間介詞，after、before、by 和 in 後接表示時間的單詞或短語，表達比較另一個時間前或後的時間。

 ## 1.3.1 怎樣用
Usage

用途

 表示某事發生在某一時間、事件或時期之後。

* after breakfast 早餐後
* after dark 天黑以後
* after the concert 演唱會過後
* after the holidays 假期以後
* She came back after a few days. 她幾天後回來了。

after 可跟 -ing 小句。

* Can you come to see me after swimming?
  你游泳之後來見我可以嗎？
* They began to be ill almost at once after eating.
  他們吃了之後幾乎馬上生病。

用途

before

表示某事發生在某一時間、事件或時期之前。

BEFORE — A POINT OF TIME — AFTER

例
- before dinner 晚飯前
- before her birthday 在她生日以前
- before October 十月前
- before the end of the year 年底以前

before 可跟 -ing 小句。

例
- I usually check my email before going to bed.
  我通常睡覺之前查一下電郵。

用途

by

指事情在某一時間之前已發生或將要發生。

BY — A POINT OF TIME

例
- by noon (不遲於中午) = at or before noon
- by Friday (在星期五或以前) = before or on Friday
- Be here by three o'clock.
  三點鐘之前來到這裏。

by 多用於 simple future tense（簡單將來式）或 future perfect tense（將來完成式）的結構。

 • Will you finish it by tomorrow?
你可以不遲於明天完成它嗎？
• The plane will arrive in Hong Kong by midnight.
航班將於午夜抵達香港。
• I shall have finished by next Wednesday.
我將在下星期三之前完成。

用途

指某事在那段時間後發生。

IN   A PERIOD OF TIME

 • in half an hour 半個小時後
• in three days 三天以後

in 一般與將來式連用，表示在某段時間以內將發生某行為。

 • I'll be ready in ten minutes.
十分鐘後我就準備好。
• They will meet us in an hour.
他們將在一小時後與我們見面。

1.3.2 注意
Notes

1) after 之後的時間如果剛好是 noon，還是要寫為 after noon。單詞 afternoon (下午) 是一個名詞，常見於介詞短語 in the afternoon。比較以下兩句：

- Come to see me after noon. 中午後來見我。
- See you in the afternoon. 下午見你。

2) after 和 before 可跟 -ing 小句，by 和 in 卻不可以。

3) after 和 before 也可用作為連接詞，後接子句。例：

- He called after you left for work this morning.
  今早你上班後他打電話來。
- Why didn't he call before I left?
  他為甚麼不在我離開之前打電話來？

4) before 也是位置介詞，另參見 2.2。

 ## 1.3.3 用法速查表
Speed check

after = later than 在……之後	before = earlier than 在……之前	by = before 不遲於、在或以前	in = after 在某段時間後
after eight 八時之後	before eight 八時之前	by eight 在八時或以前	in half an hour 半個小時後
after Monday 星期一以後	before Monday 星期一之前	by Monday 不遲於星期一	in two weeks 兩個星期以後
after Christmas 聖誕節以後	before Christmas 聖誕節之前	by Christmas 不遲於聖誕節	in a year 一年後

1.4 between, during

between 和 during 都指時間上「在⋯⋯之間」。

 ## 1.4.1 怎樣用
Usage

用途

between 指某事於一件事發生後才發生,並於另一件事發生前已經發生。

A POINT OF TIME   A POINT OF TIME

例 | • You shouldn't eat between meals. 你不應在兩餐之間吃東西。

between 多與 and 連用,表示介乎兩個時間點之間,尤其用作估計時。

例 | • What did you do between five o'clock and six o'clock?
五點到六點之間,你做了甚麼?
• The temple was built between 1830 and 1845.
這座廟宇建於 1830 年至 1845 年之間。

用途

during 指某事在某段時間裏連續發生或發生過幾次。

A PERIOD OF TIME

例 | • We went on several field trips during term break.
在學期休息期間,我們去了幾次實地考察。

用途

during 也表示某物在某段時間裏由開始到結束，都一直得到發展。

A PERIOD OF TIME

- They lived abroad during the war.
  戰爭期間他們一直住在國外。
- We go swimming every day during the summer.
  整個夏天我們每天都去游泳。

用途

during 也表示某事在某一期間內的某一刻發生。

A PERIOD OF TIME

- The old man died during the night.
  老翁在晚間死去。
- There will be a 15-minute break during the show.
  演出期間有 15 分鐘中場休息。

1.4.2 注意
Notes

1) during 用於附加狀語（adjunct），後接表示時間的名詞或名詞短語，不能後接子句。以下的說法是錯誤的：

   ✕ During I was at school, I met several nice friends.
   我在學期間，認識了幾個好朋友。

   during 後接表示時間的名詞或名詞短語，或改以連接詞 while 帶出子句：

   √ During my time at school, I met several nice friends.
   √ While I was at school, I met several nice friends.

2) between 也是位置介詞（另參見 2.7）。

1.4.3 用法速查表
Speed check

between two times or events 在⋯⋯之間	**during** a period of time 在⋯⋯期間一直
between 1939 and 1945 1939 至 1945 年間	during WWII 二次大戰期間
between 10 pm and 4 am 晚上 10 點到凌晨 4 點之間	during the night 在夜間
between 2000 and 2100 2000 至 2100 年之間	during the next 100 years 隨後一百年內

1.5 for, since

since 和 for 都表示時間長度。

 ## 1.5.1 怎樣用
Usage

用途

 **表示從過去某個具體時間起一直延續到現在。**

A POINT OF TIME

- since last week 從上週起
- since childhood 自孩提時代開始
- She has not eaten anything since breakfast.
  她自從早餐之後就沒有吃過甚麼了。
- Until last week I hadn't seen him since 1997.
  從 1997 年起直到上星期為止,我一直沒有見過他。

since 常與 present perfect tense(現在完成式)或 past perfect tense(過去完成式)連用(見上例)。如與 present tense(現在式)連用,表示重複做的事情。

- The trains run more frequently since the introduction of the new timetable.
  自從實行新的行車時間表以來,火車班次就要多一些了。

since 用於句首時起強調作用。

- Since leaving school, I have been jobless.
  自離開學校,我一直失業。

用途

for 表示某事延續，維持一段時間。

A PERIOD OF TIME

- for quite a while 好一會兒
- for several days 好幾天
- She has not eaten anything for hours.
  她已幾個小時沒有進食了。
- Until last week I hadn't seen him for almost twenty years.
  到上星期為止，我差不多二十年沒有見過他。

for 多與 present perfect tense（現在完成式）或 past perfect tense（過去完成式）連用（見上例），但也可與任何時態同用。

- Bake the cake for 30 minutes.
  把蛋糕烘 30 分鐘。
- We chatted for quite a while.
  我們聊了好一會兒。

for 用於句首時起強調作用。

- For years John was unable to find a girlfriend.
  約翰好幾年沒能找到女朋友。

1.5.2 注意
Notes

1） since 表示一段時間的開始，for 表示一段時間。比較以下兩句：

- They have lived in Sydney since 1996.
  1996 年起他們就住在悉尼了。
- They have lived in Sydney (for)* almost twenty years.
  他們住在悉尼已接近二十年了。

* for 偶爾可以刪去，而 since 絕不能省略。

2） 在否定詞或最高級之後，英國人用 for，美國人可能用 in。例如：

- （英）She had not eaten a good meal for a long time.
- （美）She had not eaten a good meal in a long time.
  她好久沒吃過一頓豐富的飯了。

3） since 除了是時間介詞，還可以是連接詞，後接子句。例：

- She has been very busy since she started her own business.
  她自從開始自己的生意以來，一直很瘦。

for 也可用作連接詞，後接子句，表示原因，與時間無關。例：

- She found it difficult to read, for her eyes were failing.
  她閱讀時感到吃力，因為視力大不如前了。

1.5.3 用法速查表
Speed check

for	since
a period (from start to end) 一段時間	a point of time (up to now) 一段時間的開始
for 20 minutes 達二十分鐘	since 10 am 從早上十點開始
for hours 達幾個小時	since breakfast 自從早餐以後
for three days 達三天	since Monday 從星期一起
for thirty years 達三十年	since 1997 自 1997 年以來
for two centuries 達兩個世紀	since January 自一月份開始
for a long time 很長一段時間	since I left school 我離開學校以後
for ever 永遠	since the beginning of time 自從
all tenses 可與不同時態連用	perfect tenses usually 多與完成式連用

1.6　till, until

till 和 until 用於一個時間點之前，表示「直到（某時為止）」，兩者可以互換使用。

 ## 1.6.1 怎樣用
Usage

用途

 A 表示某事發生，並且直到某一時刻才結束。

A POINT OF TIME

例
- Wait till I call. 等着我打電話來。
- They have to wait till winter. 他們要等到冬季。
- This shop opens until midnight. 這家商店營業至午夜。

用途

B 指事情到某一時刻才發生。用在附加狀語裏，常與否定小句連用。

A POINT OF TIME

例
- He doesn't go to bed until midnight. 直到午夜，他才上牀睡覺。
- I'm afraid we won't meet again till next January.
  恐怕我們在明年一月之前也不會再見面。

until 可用於句首，起強調作用，till 則不可以。

 • Until when does this supermarket stay open?
這超市營業到幾點？
• Until her accident, she had always been strong and healthy.
她在那次意外之前身體一直很健壯。

與 from 連用表示「從……到……」，與 to 同義。

 • They stayed from Tuesday until / till Saturday.
他們從星期二住到星期六。

 ## 1.6.2 注意
Notes

1) 注意 till 和 until 的正確拼寫：

T-I-L-L for till (not til)

U-N-T-I-L for until (not untill)

2) until 比 till 的語氣稍微正式一點。till 多用於報章、廣告、歌詞等，
簡寫作 'til，也多見於約定俗成的套語中，例如 shop 'til you drop、It
ain't over 'til it's over 或 'Til we meet again。

3) till 和 until 除了是時間介詞，還可以是連接詞，後接子句。

 • They have to wait till the results are announced this winter.
他們要等到結果在今年冬天公佈。
• The shopkeepers work hard until the shop closes at midnight.
直到商店在午夜關門，店主還在努力工作。

4) 小心不要混淆 until 和 by（另參見 1.3.1 by 的用法）。比較以下兩句：

 • The plane will not arrive in Hong Kong until midnight.
該航班要到半夜才抵達香港。
• The plane will not arrive in Hong Kong by midnight.
該航班將不會在半夜或以前抵達香港。

1.6.3 用法速查表
Speed check

till / until = up to the time that 直到（某一刻）為止
till / until five 直到五點為止
till / until Christmas 直到聖誕節為止
to postpone the meeting till / until Friday 把會議推遲到星期五舉行
以下慣用短語屬於例外，用 to 不用 till / until
to the last 直到最後；至死：I kept trying to the last. 我一直堅持到底。
to this day 直到現在：The tradition continues to this day. 那項傳統保存至今。
to date 到目前為止：I emailed you two weeks ago, but to date I've not received a reply. 我兩星期前給你發了電郵，但到目前為止還沒有收到你的回覆。

02 PREPOSITIONS FOR PLACE 位置介詞

表示位置關係的介詞大致可分以下十類。

2.1 at, on, in

一般來説，at 代表在「一點」的位置， on 代表在比「一點」大的位置，而 in 則代表在更大的地方。

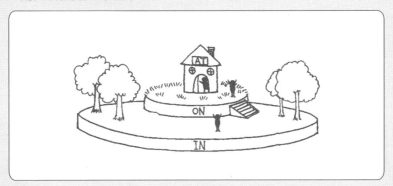

⚡ 2.1.1 怎樣用
Usage

用途

at 指處於某地方，用於特定的定點位置、相對細小的空間。

- at home 在家裏
- at the corner 在拐角處
- at the entrance 在入口處
- Jane is waiting for you at the bus stop.
  珍正在巴士站那裏等你。
- The shop is at the end of the street. 商店在街道盡頭。

特定的定點位置還包括 at the table / at the door 、 at the top / at the bottom 、 at work / at school / at university 等。

用途

on

指「在……表面上」，用於平面和比一點為大的空間。

- on the ground 在地上
- on page seven 在第七頁
- on the carpet 在地毯上
- on stage 在舞台上
- The author's name is on the cover of the book.
  作者名字在圖書封面上。
- There are no prices on this menu. 這份餐牌沒有標示價錢。
- There was a "no smoking" sign on the wall.
  牆上貼有「不准吸煙」的告示。

平面的空間還包括 on your face、on the floor、on a table、on the grass 等，但以下情況則屬例外，用 in 不用 on：in a mirror、in bed、in the newspaper 等。

用途

in

指「在某處」，用於圍住的或相對來說更大的空間。

- in the garden 在花園裏
- in the office 在辦公室裏
- in China 在中國
- Do you live in Taipei? 你是住在台北嗎？
- Jupiter is in the Solar System. 木星位於太陽系內。

圍住的空間還包括一些交通工具，例如 in a car / taxi / helicopter / boat 等，但以下情況則屬例外，用 on 不用 in：
on a bus / train / plane / ship / bicycle / motorbike、on a horse / an elephant 等。

比較中英文

位置介詞的細化分類程度高於漢字，at、on 和 in 同樣表示方位，在英語裏有細微差別，但中文一律用「在……」表示。

2.1.2 注意
Notes

1) 比較 at、on 和 in 的用法：

- He lives at 188, King's Road. 他住在英皇道 188 號。
  （用於特定地點之前，通常指位置、地址、建築物、村莊或小城鎮）
- He lives on King's Road. 他住在英皇道（那條街上）。
  （用於指街道名稱）
- He lives in Hong Kong. 他住在香港。
  （用於重要城鎮、都市、國家或任何大地區的名稱之前）

多看一例：

- Mr. Brown lives on the 6th floor at 32 Oxford Street in London.
  布朗先生住在倫敦牛津街 32 號六樓。

2) at、on、in 也是時間介詞，另參見 1.1。

2.1.3 用法速查表
Speed check

at for a point 定點位置、相對細小的 空間	on for a surface 平面、比一點為大的空間	in for an enclosed space 圍住的、大的空間
at the corner	on page seven	in a box
at the entrance	on the wall	in my pocket
at the bus stop	on the carpet	in the garden
at the top of the page	on the ceiling	in the office
at the end of the road	on the ground	in a car
at the crossroads*	on the floor	in a building
at the front desk	on the menu	in her hometown
at the peak	on stage	in China
以下短語屬於例外：		
	on a bus	in a car
	on a train	in a taxi
	on a plane	in a helicopter
	on a ship	in a boat
	on a bicycle, on a motorbike	in the newspaper
	on a horse, on an elephant	in bed
	on the radio, on television	in the mirror

*crossroads: 十字路口

2.2 in front of, behind

in front of 和 behind 是表示前後的位置介詞。

| I am standing in front of my cat. | I am standing behind my cat. |

 ## 2.2.1 怎樣用
Usage

用途

in front of 指在人、物或地點之前。

例
- in front of Paul 在保羅前面
- in front of the blackboard 在黑板前面
- A boy ran out in front of the bus. 有個男孩從巴士前面跑出來。
- I couldn't watch the TV because she was standing in front of the screen. 我無法看電視,因為她站在熒幕的正前面。

用途

behind 指在人、物或地點之後。

例
- behind the curtains 在窗簾之後
- behind the bank 在銀行後面
- She's standing behind the post. 她站在燈柱後面。
- A boy ran out from behind a tree. 男孩從樹後跑出來。
- The man shut the door behind him. 那人把身後的門關上。

2.2.2 注意
Notes

1) in front of 作為一個介詞短語，of 是必須的。否則它便用作副詞，解作「前面」。

> **例**
> - The washroom is in front. 洗手間在前面。
> - The car in front stopped suddenly. 前面的車突然停了下來。

2) 比較 in front of 和另一個介詞短語 in / at the front of。

> **例**
> - A boy ran out in front of the bus. 有個男孩從巴士前面跑出來。
> - The boy took a seat in / at the front of the bus.
>   那個男孩在巴士上的靠前座位坐下來。

3) behind 除了是介詞，還可作副詞用。

> **例**
> - The house has a huge garden behind.
>   房子後面有一個很大的花園。

4) 介詞 before 與 in front of 同義，都指「在……前面」，in front of 用於一般場合，而 before 用於文學與正式場合，例如法庭審訊和教堂裏的儀式等。

> **例**
> - The accused man was brought before the magistrate.
>   被告被帶到了裁判官面前。
> - The priest stood before the altar. 那個神父站在聖壇前面。

5) 介詞 after 不是位置介詞，不能取代 behind。after someone 指在某人離開後為他做某事，與 behind someone（在某人後面）的意思不同。

> **例**
> - He went and closed the door behind her.
>   他過去關上她身後的門。
> - He went and closed the door after her.
>   他在她走後過去關上門。

2.2.3 用法速查表
Speed check

The smaller pupils sit	**in front of** = in the position directly before 在……之前	the taller ones.
The singers stand		the audience.
Don't stand		the screen.
The taller students sit	**behind** = at or towards the back of 在……之後	the smaller ones.
The band sits		the singers.
Hide yourself		the screen.

2.3　on the left of, on the right of

on the left of　和 on the right of 是表示左右的位置介詞。

| I am standing on the left of my cat. | I am standing on the right of my cat. |

2.3.1 怎樣用
Usage

用途

on the left of　指人或物在⋯⋯的左邊。

- on the left of the cinema 戲院的左邊
- The winners were sitting on the left of the headmaster.
  得獎者坐在校長的左邊。
- Our school is on the left of the main road.
  我們的學校在大馬路的左邊。

用途

on the right of 指人或物在……的右邊。

- on the right of Mary 在瑪莉的右邊
- There is a swimming pool on the right of the aviary.
  百鳥居的右邊有個游泳池。
- The library was on the right of the main building, and the canteen was on the left.
  圖書館在本部大樓右邊，飯堂在左邊。

on the right of Mary

2.3.2 注意
Notes

1) on the left / right of 也作 to the left / right of。

- There is a swimming pool to/on the right of the aviary.
  百鳥居右邊有個游泳池。
- The murderer was sitting to/on the left of a policeman.
  那名殺人犯坐在警員左邊。

2) left 和 right 都擁有多重詞性,既是名詞(on the right),又是形容詞 (your left arm)和副詞(turn right)。另外,它們又用來比喻政治立場, left 和 right 解作「左 / 右翼、左 / 右傾」,用作名詞時則解作「左 / 右 派政黨」。

2.3.3 用法速查表
Speed check

The bank is	**on the left of** = on the opposite side to the hand that most people write with 在……的左邊	the office building.
The singers stand		the audience.
The girls sit	**on the right of** = on the side to the hand that most people write with 在……的右邊	the boys.
The band sits		the singers.

2.4 above, over, below, under, at the top of, at the bottom of

above / below、over / under 和 at the top of / at the bottom of 都是表示上下的位置介詞。

The butterflies are flying above the flowers.

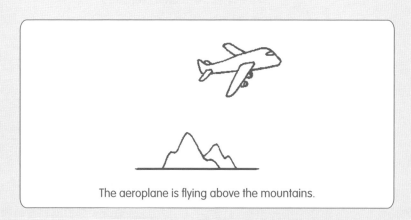

The aeroplane is flying above the mountains.

2.4.1 怎樣用
Usage

用途

above, over ▸ 指某物高於另一事物或在另一事物的上方。

The birds are flying above me.

- above / over your head 你的頭上
- above / over the valley 山谷上

兩者同樣指在「在……上方（但不接觸表面）」。在以下例句中，兩者常可互相替代。

- A sign hung above / over the door. 門的上方掛着一塊招牌。
- The birds flew above / over the trees. 鳥兒在樹叢上方飛翔。
- There is an owl on the branch above / over you.
  在你頭頂上方的樹枝上有一隻貓頭鷹。

不過，over 也有「直接在……之上」的意思，帶有覆蓋表面的含義。而 above 僅表示「高於……」的意思，沒有覆蓋表面的含義。在以下例句中，絕對不能用 above 替代 over。

• Grass is growing over the roof. 屋頂長滿了草。
• The magician put a mask over his face. 魔術師戴上了面具。

用途

below, under 指某物低於另一事物或在另一事物的下方。

在以下例句中，兩者常可互相替代。

 • below / under your eyes　在你雙眼之下
• below / under the blanket　在毯子之下
• We sheltered below / under the tree.　我們躲在樹下。
• Below us on the right there is the mighty River Nile.
　我們右下方是浩瀚的尼羅河。

不過，below 不總是可以替代 under，因為 below 僅表示「低於……」的意思，under 則意味着「在……的正下方」之意，例如表示某物被一層東西（如衣服）覆蓋着。在以下例句中，絕對不能用 below 替代 under。

 • That man has a gun under his cloak.
　那男人在大衣下藏着一支手槍。
• Under the film of fat, the sausages are pink.
　粉紅香腸上薄薄覆蓋着一層脂肪。

用途

at the top of, at the bottom of

也表示上下位置。

I am at the top of the pyramid. My friends are at the bottom of the pyramid.

at the top of 指在某事物的頂部或上端。

- at the top of the hill 在山頂上
- at the top of the ferris wheel 在摩天輪最上端
- My name was at the top of the list. 我的名字在名單的上端。
- I saw a woman standing at the top of IFC yesterday.
  昨天我看見一個女人站在國際金融大廈的屋頂上。

at the bottom of 指在某事物的底部或下端。

- at the bottom of the page 書頁下端
- at the bottom of the sea 在海底
- I eventually found my wedding ring at the bottom of my bag.
  我終於在提包底找到我的結婚指環。
- The body was found at the bottom of a deserted well.
  屍體在一口荒井的井底找到了。

2.4.2 注意
Notes

介詞 beneath 和 underneath 可以替代 below 和 under，同樣表達「在……下方」的意思，但它們的文學色彩較重，用於比較正式的場合。

• beneath the pale moonlight 蒼白的月色下
• underneath your clothes 你的衣服底下

 ## 2.4.3 用法速查表
Speed check

above / over		at the top of
= higher than, but not touching 在……之上		= at the highest part of 在……的頂部
above / over your head 在你的頭頂上		at the top of the page 在書頁上端
above / over the bridge 在橋上		at the top of the mountain 山頂上
	= resting on top of 直接在……之上、覆蓋着	
	cloth over the bread 布覆蓋着麵包	
below / under		at the bottom of
= lower than, but not touching 在……之下		= at the lowest part of 在……的底部
below / under your eyes 在你雙眼之下		at the bottom of the sea 在海底
below / under the tree 在樹下		at the bottom of the list 在名單的下端
	= coverd by 直接在……之下、被覆蓋的	
	a sick child under the blanket 被毯子覆蓋着的病童	

2.5 beside, by, close to, near, next to

beside、by、close to、near 和 next to 都是表示「在⋯⋯旁邊」的位置介詞。

⚡ 2.5.1 怎樣用
Usage

用途

表示在某人或物的一邊，尤指緊挨着某人或物。

My cat is sitting beside / by / next to me.

beside

- beside me 在我身旁
- a small town beside the sea 海邊的小城鎮
- He usually sits beside the driver. 他通常坐在司機身旁。

by

- by your side 在你身邊
- Sit by me. 挨着我坐吧。
- the pot plant by the window 窗旁的盆栽植物
- The old man wished to be buried by his wife.
  那老人希望葬在他妻子墳旁。

next to

- next to the railway 鐵路旁邊
- the bank next to the old cinema 舊戲院旁的銀行
- The music room is next to the computer room.
  音樂室在電腦室旁邊。

用途

close to 和 near

則指某物在另一事物的附近。

My cat is sitting close to / near me.

close to

- close to the border 靠近邊界
- They sat close to the bonfire to keep warm.
  他們坐在火堆旁取暖。
- I'm in a café close to the Cultural Centre.
  我在文化中心附近的一家咖啡館裏。

near

- near the door 門旁
- an apartment near an MTR station 靠近港鐵站的一套住房
- There is a new shopping mall near our school.
  學校附近蓋了一座新購物商場。

2.5.2 注意
Notes

1) 不要混淆 beside 與 besides。beside 指 at the side of，即「在……旁邊」，besides 則指 in addition to 或 as well as，即「除……以外（還）」。比較以下兩個例子：

- Please stay beside her. 請留在她身邊。
- Please stay besides her.
  除了她以外，（你們其餘各位）請留下。

2) close to 有比較形式 closer 和最高級形式 closest。

- They want to live closer to the city. 他們想住得靠近城市一點。
- Shenzhen is closest to Hong Kong. 深圳最接近香港。

3) near 也有比較形式 nearer 和最高級形式 nearest。

- We want to find an apartment nearer the harbour.
  我們想找能靠近海港一點的套房。

4) near 也用 near to 的形式，但大部份情況下都是單獨使用。而 next 和 close 卻不能單獨用作介詞，必須與 to 連用，即 next to 和 close to。

- Please stay near (to) her. 請留在她身邊。
- Please stay next to her. 請留在她身邊。
- Please stay close to her. 請靠近她。

5) near 也作副詞用。例：

- The post office is quite near. 郵局很近。

2.5.3 用法速查表
Speed check

beside / by / next to = at the side of 在……旁邊	close to / near = not at much distance away 在……附近
beside / by / next to me 挨着我	close to / near me 在我身旁
beside / by / next to the door 門旁	close to / near the door 門的不遠處
beside / by / next to the railway 鐵路旁邊	close to / near the railway 鐵路附近

2.6 inside, outside

inside 和 outside 分別表示內外的位置。

2.6.1 怎樣用
Usage

用途

inside > 指人、物、動物在某空間或處所內，該空間不少於一方被封閉。

I am inside the box. | I jump outside the box.

例
- inside the room 在房間內
- inside your cup 在你的杯子內
- Put the money inside your wallet. 把錢放進你的錢包內。
- We were waiting inside the cinema. 我們在電影院裏面等着。

用途

outside

指人、物、動物在不少一方被封閉的空間之外。

 例

- outside the hall 在禮堂外
- outside the window 窗外
- The children are playing outside the door.
  那些孩子正在門外玩。
- The shop outside our school sells limited edition collectibles.
  學校外邊那家商店出售限量版收藏品。

 ## 2.6.2 注意
Notes

1) inside 和 in 同義，但使用 inside 時側重於一些空間的一側被封鎖的客觀環境。比較以下兩句：

(1) The children are in the classroom. 孩子在課室內。

(2) Don't eat inside the classroom. 在課室之內切勿進食。

雖然把兩個句子寫成 The children are inside the classroom. 和 Don't eat in the classroom. 也未嘗不可以，但原句 (1) 純粹指出孩子現時身處何方，重點不落在他們被困在班房這四面牆之內的客觀環境。而 (2) 所強調的是「在課室內不可進食，但在課室這四面以外的地方（如操場、禮堂等）卻沒有此限制。

2) 在非正式英語，尤其在美式英語中，可用 inside of 和 outside of。

例

- I've known him for years, but I've never been inside of his house.
  我認識他多年，但我從未到過他家。
- Put it outside of the classroom. 將它放在課室外。

3) inside 和 outside 都可作副詞用：

例

- Children are not allowed to go inside. 兒童不准入內。
- It was raining hard outside. 外面雨下得很大。

4) inside 和 within 都能表示被某物體圍住的意思，但 inside 比較通用，within 則比較正式，而且主要用於大範圍（比較 inside a box / within the museum）。

 ## 2.6.3 用法速查表
Speed check

inside = within 在⋯⋯的裏面	outside = not in something, but near it 在⋯⋯的外面
inside the bin 垃圾桶內	outside the bin 垃圾桶外
inside his wallet 在他的錢包內	outside his wallet 在他的錢包外
inside the kitchen 在廚房內	outside the kitchen 在廚房外
inside the fence 圍欄內	outside the fence 圍欄外

2.7 between, among

介詞 between 和 among 都表示「在……中間」的意思。

I am standing between two chairs.

⚡ 2.7.1 怎樣用
Usage

用途

between 表示人或物處於兩個事物之間或連接於兩者的直線上。

 例
- between Peter and Mary 在彼得和瑪麗中間
- somewhere in between Hong Kong and Shenzhen
  在香港和深圳之間的某個地方
- Her body was firmly wedged between the two rocks.
  她的身體被牢牢地嵌在兩塊岩石中間。
- He put the cigarette between his lips and lit it.
  他把香煙銜在嘴唇之間，點上了火。

between 用於句首時起強調作用。

 例
- Between my shoulders I had a severe pain.
  在雙肩之間，我覺得痛死了。

用途

among

表示某事物或某人處於或活動於某些事物或人中間。

- among high mountains 在崇山峻嶺中
- The tower is hidden among tall trees.
  那座塔隱藏在高高的樹林中。
- The little girl was lost among the crowd.
  那小孩在人群中消失了。

among 用於句首時起強調作用。

- Among the books he found one by his grandfather.
  在書堆之中，他發現了祖父的著作。

Among the five students, three of them wear purple T-shirts.

2.7.2 注意
Notes

1) between you and me 或 between ourselves 是慣用口語，指「你我私下說說，不讓其他人知道」，與位置無關。

 • Between you and me, Tom's rather stupid.
這是我們私下裏說的話，湯姆這個人很蠢。

2) among 也作 amongst，但 amongst 是書面語。

3) among (amongst) 後必須接複數的名詞或代名詞。

 • among the books / rocks / mountains
書堆中 / 山岩中 / 崇山峻嶺間
• among the crowd / unemployed / elderly
人群中 / 失業人口之中 / 長者之間

 ## 2.7.3 用法速查表
Speed check

between = in the middle of two persons or things 在（兩者）之間	among = in the middle of three or more persons or things 在（團體、人群等）當中
between Peter and Mary 在彼德和瑪莉之間	among the crowd 在人群當中
between the two children 在兩名孩童之間	among the four children 在四個孩子當中
between my lips 兩唇之間	among the hair 毛髮之間
between Hong Kong and Taiwan 在香港和台灣之間	among the countries 國與國之間

2.8 opposite, across from

介詞 opposite 和 across from 都表示「在⋯⋯對面」的意思。

My friend is just opposite me.

⚡ 2.8.1 怎樣用
Usage

用途

opposite 和 across from 指某物在另一物的對面。

- opposite /across from the building 在建築物對面
- The bus stop is just opposite / across from our school.
  巴士站正好在我們的學校對面。
- The shop opposite / across from our office sells replicas and knock-offs.
  我們辦公室對面的那家商店賣冒牌貨和山寨版。

opposite 之後有時可接 to。

- He missed those days when he lived opposite to her.
  他懷念住在她對面的那段日子。

opposite 用於句首時起強調作用。

- Opposite the police station is a building with many one-woman brothels.
  警察局對面的那棟大樓裏有不少一樓一妓院。

2.8.2 注意
Notes

1) opposite 之後可加 to，但並不常見，而 across from 的 from 在任何情況下都不能省略。以下三句都正確。

   - Jane lives opposite to Bob.
   - Jane lives opposite Bob.
   - Jane lives across from Bob.（not lives across Bob）

2) opposite 和 to 不能拆開來用，但 across from 卻可以。

   ✓ A is opposite (to) B.
   ✗ A is opposite (the street/table etc) to B.
   ✓ A is across from B.
   ✓ A is across (the street/table etc) from B.

3) opposite 除了是介詞以外，還是形容詞、副詞和名詞。作為一個介詞，opposite 不會和 of 同用，更鮮與 to 同用。但作為一個名詞或形容詞時，它經常與 of 或 to 連用。

   - （名詞）Wealth is the opposite of poverty.
     財富是貧窮的相反。
   - （形容詞）His room is opposite to hers.
     他的房間在她那間對面。

2.8.3 用法速查表
Speed check

---

opposite, across from
= facing; = to or on the opposite side of
在……對面

---

opposite / across from the table 在桌子的對面

---

opposite / across from our school 在我們的學校對面

---

opposite / across from the police station 在警察局對面

2.9 across, against, alongside

介詞 across、against 和 alongside 分別是「靠倚着」和「並排」的意思。

 2.9.1 **怎樣用**
Usage

用途

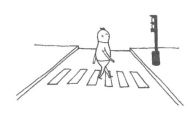

across 指某物滿佈或橫跨另一物或平面。

I am walking across the road.

- a crack across the ceiling 天花上的一道縫隙
- a banner across the street 一條懸過馬路的橫幅
- She lay across the bed. 她橫躺在牀上。
- Printed across the sign was the word "DANGER".
  告示上印着「危險」字樣。

用途

against

是指某物或人靠倚着另一物或平面。

I am leaning against the wall.

- against the wall　靠牆
- against a tree　倚傍着一棵樹
- The boys are pressing their noses against the window.
  那些男孩把鼻子緊貼在窗子上。

I am leaning against the tree.

用途

alongside

指某物在另一事物的旁邊，有「順着或靠着……旁邊」、「與…並排」的意思。

I am running alongside my friend.

- Little Tim ran alongside his father. 小添跟在他爸爸旁邊跑。
- We brought our boat alongside their boat.
  我們把船靠到他們的船旁邊。
- There is a brothel alongside the church. 教堂旁邊有一家妓院。
- A bus suddenly stopped alongside her.
  巴士忽然在她身邊停下。
- He parked his car alongside the parking meter.
  他把車停在停車收費器旁邊。

The woman walked alongside her husband.

2.9.2 注意
Notes

across 也是方向介詞，參見 3.6。

2.9.3 用法速查表
Speed check

across = from one side to the other of 橫過	**against** = touching esp. for support 靠倚着	**alongside** = next to; along the side of 順着或靠着……旁邊； 與……並排
across the fence 在圍欄對面	against the fence 倚靠着圍欄	a boat alongside their boat 靠到他們的船旁邊的船
opposite a lamppost 在燈柱對面	against a lamppost 倚靠着燈柱	a brothel alongside the church 教堂旁邊的一家妓院
opposite your head 在玻璃板對面	against the glass panel 倚靠着玻璃板	a bus alongside her 她身邊的巴士

2.10 down, off

介詞 down 和 off 都指某事物在一段距離以外的位置。

⚡ 2.10.1 怎樣用
Usage

用途

down 指在⋯⋯的下方。

例
- The washroom is down those stairs. 洗手間在那樓梯下面。
- See the sentence halfway down the page?
  看到這一頁中間的那個句子嗎?

down 也指在⋯⋯的那一端。

例
- We live just down the road. 我們就住在道路的那一頭。
- There is a bridge a mile down the river from here.
  從這裏沿河往下一英里處有一座橋。

用途

off 指離開(海岸、街道)一段距離的位置。

例
- just off the shore 距離海岸不遠的海面
- ten miles off the Diaoyu Islands 離釣魚台十公里的海面
- a narrow street off Nathan Road
  從彌敦道拐進去的一條狹窄小街
- The supermarket is just 30 metres off the main road.
  超級市場離開大馬路只有三十米。

2.10.2 注意
Notes

down 也是方向介詞，參見 3。

2.10.3 用法速查表
Speed check

down = in a lower place in; at the far end of 在⋯⋯的下方；在⋯⋯的那一端	**off** = (of a road) turning away from; in the sea near (指道路) 離開；靠近⋯⋯的海面
down the stairs 在樓梯底下	100 feet off Nathan Road 離開彌敦道 100 尺以外
down the road 在道路的那一頭	an island off the coast 海岸附近的一個島嶼

表示方向關係的介詞大致可分以下六類。

I am walking away from home.　I am walking towards home.

3.1　from, to, away from, towards

一般來說，from 和 away from 指從某處來，to 和 towards 指到某目的地或達至目標。

 3.1.1 **怎樣用**
　　　　　Usage

用途

 **指人或物離開某處到別的地方。**

例 • I got a parcel from my ex-girlfriend yesterday.
　　昨天我收到前女友寄來的一個包裹。
　 • She took her iPad from her handbag.　她從手袋裏取出 iPad。

用途

from 後面常接某人的出生地、或某物的產地或發源地。

- He comes from Sydney. 他來自雪梨。
- Can you name a composer from China?
  你能說出一個中國作曲家的名字嗎？

用途

to 後面是一個目的地或者目標。

- a visit to the museum 去參觀博物館
- on a journey to Africa 去非洲的旅途上
- She went to the library. 她去了圖書館。
- She goes to church every Sunday morning.
  她每個星期天早上去教堂。
- This bus will take us to the Peak. 這巴士會帶我們到山頂。

用途

to 有「朝、向」的意思，與 towards 一樣。

- She went to the library. 她到圖書館去了。
- She goes to church every Sunday morning.
  她逢週日早上去教會。

用途

away from 和 towards

的重點，在於行動或動作的特定方向，而不是行動或動作的結果或者目標。

away from 指某人或物離開某處，往別的地方去。

- I walked away from a tree. 我從樹下走開。
- They walked away from the temple. 他們離開了廟宇。
- They swan away from land. 他們從陸地游了出去。
- She pulled away from him and jumped into the river.
  她掙開他，然後跳進河裏。

towards 表示朝某人或物的方向移動、觀看或指點。

- She looks back towards me. 她回過頭來看着我。
- The man gestured towards the waitress.
  那男人向女服務員打手勢。
- A butterfly is flying towards me.
  一隻蝴蝶正向着我的方向飛來。
- The car is moving towards the cliff. 汽車正朝着懸崖方向駛去。

The butterfly is flying towards me.

3.1.2 注意
Notes

1) from 和 to 經常連用,表達「從(某個地方)到(某個地方)」的意思。

- The Island Line runs from Kennedy Town to Chai Wan.
  港島線由堅尼地城行駛至柴灣。
- It takes ten minutes to go from the bus stop to the beach.
  由巴士站到海灘,需時十分鐘。

2) from 與 to 也是時間介詞,參見 1.2。此外, from 也是計算介詞,參見 9.3。

3) to 與東南西北或左右等方位詞連用,以表明某事物所處的位置。

- to the north of Hong Kong 港島以北
- Keep to the left. 靠左邊走。
- Take the next turning to your right. 下個拐彎處右轉。
- The airport is a few kilometres to the west of the city.
  機場位於城市西面數公里。

4) to 和 towards 有時可以互相替換使用,但如果思想上強調向某具體方向移動,則用 towards 較 to 好。

- He ran away when he felt that someone was coming towards him.
  他感到有人正向他這邊走過來,於是他逃跑了。

5) 在美式英語中, towards 會拼寫成 toward。

3.1.3 用法速查表
Speed check

from = starting at 自……；從自……（表示起點的地點、位置等）	to = in the direction of 往（某個目的地、目標）去
from Sheung Wan 從上環	to Kennedy Town 往堅尼地城
from the park 從公園	to the Peak 往山頂
from New York 從紐約	to London 往倫敦
blowing from the ocean 從海洋吹來	blowing to the land 吹入陸地
away from = leaving 離開（某處、某物或某人）	**towards** = in the direction of 朝（某個方向）去
away from the West 離開西方	towards the East 朝東方走
far away from war 遠離戰爭	a step towards peace 邁向和平的一步
away from the main road 離開大馬路	towards the end of the alley 朝小巷盡頭
away from land 離開陸地	towards the sea 向海

3.2 into, out of

into 和 out of 表示「進入」和「離開」兩個相反方向。

I am walking into the lift.   I am walking out of the lift.

 ## 3.2.1 怎樣用
Usage

用途

into 指從外面進入一個圍起的空間裏。

- into the tunnel 進入隧道
- into the river 進河裏
- We walked into the cinema. 我們走進電影院。
- The little boy jumps into the sea. 小男孩跳入海裏。
- The waiter is pouring some water into the glass.
  侍應正把水倒進玻璃杯內。

用途

out of 指離開一個圍起的空間，走到外面。

- Get out of my room right now! 馬上離開我的房間！
- Dont throw rubbish out of the window. 不要把垃圾扔到窗外。

3.2.2 注意
Notes

1) 雖然 into 和 out of 均可以分拆成兩個單字，但前者拼寫成一個單字，而後者則是兩個單字。

2) into 不一定是方向介詞，而它另一個意思是「轉變成為」。

- The teacher turned the empty cans and bottles into a piece of art.
  老師把空罐和空樽變成一件藝術品。
- The professor can translate ten different languages into Chinese.
  教授可以把十種不同語言翻譯成中文。

3) 在日常會話中，into 有時也用來表示「非常有興趣」的意思。

- Are you into martial art? 你對武術有興趣嗎？
- He's very much into archaeology. 他對考古學興趣甚濃。

4) out of 也是表示計算的介詞，參見 9.4。

5) out of 亦常見於不少的慣用短語，包括：out of curiosity（出於好奇），out of danger（脫離危險），out of wood（用木材製造），out of petrol（汽油耗盡），out of action（失靈；發生故障），out of breath（喘不過氣來），out of character（出人意料），out of date（已不流行），out of print（不再發行），out of sight（在視線範圍以外），out of work（失業），out of the blue（意外地），out of the ordinary（不平凡），out of the question（不可能），out of the woods（脫離險境）等。

3.2.3 用法速查表
Speed check

into	out of
= so as to be inside (something) 從外面進入	= so as to be outside (something) 離開一個圍起的空間
into the sea （跳）入海中	out of my room 離開我的房間
into the glass （倒）進玻璃杯內	out of the window （扔）到窗外
into Room 903 （進）入 903 號房	out of a pocket 從袋中（取）出
into a bank account （存）入銀行帳戶裏	out of the trap 從陷阱中（逃）出

3.3 on to, off

on to 和 off 是表示踏上和離開一個平面的方向介詞。

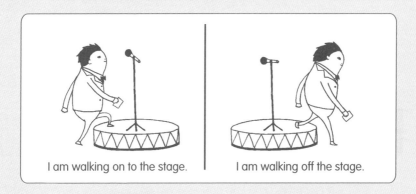

I am walking on to the stage. | I am walking off the stage.

 ## 3.3.1 怎樣用
Usage

用途

on to （也作 onto）指向一個平面移上。

例
- We climbed on to a rock. 我們爬到一塊岩石上。
- The skater stepped on to the ice. 溜冰手踩到冰上去。
- A fly landed on to the dining table. 一隻蒼蠅降落在餐桌上。
- Little Judy climbed on to her father's lap.
  小茱迪爬上她父親的腿上。
- Jack hops on to his new bicycle in no time.
  傑克立即跳上他的新自行車。
- The car crashed on to the pavement.
  汽車撞上了人行道。

用途

on to 後接交通工具表示上車、上飛機等。

- He jumped on to the train. 他跳上了火車。
- She hurled herself on to the bus. 她縱身跳上了巴士。

用途

off 指「離開（一個平面）」。

例
- They walked off the stage. 他們步下舞台。
- Get off the chair and do some work!
  離開椅子，做些工作吧！
- She slowly lifted her elbows off the dining table.
  她慢慢把手肘移離餐桌。
- Lift the cup off the saucer. 把茶杯從茶碟上拿起。
- We should keep off the grass. 我們不應該踐踏草地。

用途

off 後接交通工具表示下車、下飛機等。

- We got off the train at Sheung Shui. 我們在上水站下了火車。
- The first boy off the bus was Justin.
  第一個下巴士的男孩是賈斯丁。

3.3.2 注意
Notes

1) on to 為複合介詞,在很多場合下既可分寫成兩詞 (on to),也可合寫成一詞(即 onto,儘管這個用法現正逐漸罕見)。不過,當 on 是短語動詞 (phrasal verb) 的一部份(即介副詞)時,on to 必須分寫。

例 | • Please move on to the next point of discussion.
請繼續討論下一點。

× Please move onto the next point of discussion.

2) off 不單是後接名詞短語或代名詞的介詞,也是副詞 (adverb),亦常與之前的動詞形成一個短語動詞 (phrasal verb)。

例 | • The eyelashes of the doll often fall off. 洋娃娃的睫毛常常掉落。
• The last flight took off at midnight. 最後一班航機午夜起飛。
• The handle of the window has come off. 窗口的手柄脫落了。
• He has run off with a girl. 他與一個女孩私奔了。

3) off 也是位置介詞,參見 2.10。

 ## 3.3.3 用法速查表
Speed check

onto = to a place 到(一個平面)上面	**off** = away from a place 離開(一個平面)
onto the dining table(降落)在餐桌上	off the chair 離開椅子
onto his lap(爬)上他的腿上	off the dining table(移)離餐桌
onto a bicycle(跳)上自行車	off the saucer 從茶碟上(拿)起
onto the pavement(撞)上了人行道	off the grass 離開草地

3.4 up, down

up 和 down 分別表示「由下而上」和「由上而下」兩個相反方向。

I am walking up the stairs.　　I am walking down the stairs.

3.4.1 怎樣用
Usage

用途

up ▶ 表示向上移動，例如上樓梯、爬梯子、上坡等。

例
- The cat ran up the tree. 貓兒跑到樹上去。
- He is going up the stairs. 他正在上樓梯。
- The firefighter quickly climbed up the ladder and rescued the little boy. 那名消防員迅速爬上雲梯，救了小男孩出來。

也表示沿着道路行走，或逆水而上的方向走。

例
- She walked up the footpath slowly. 她在小徑緩慢向上走。
- The bank is just two blocks up the road.
  銀行在路那頭兩個街區遠的地方。
- When you go up the river, don't hit the rocks.
  你逆水而上時，小心不要觸礁。

用途

down

表示向下移動，例如下樓梯、爬下梯子、沿着山坡往下走等。

例
- go down the slide
  從滑梯滑下來
- The trolley was sliding down the slope.
  手推車正在斜坡上滑下來。

也表示沿着道路向對面走去，或順着水流的方向走。

例
- We went down the country lane for a few miles.
  我們沿着鄉間小道走了幾英里。
- The raft floated down the stream.
  木筏漂流而下。

3.4.2 注意
Notes

以下句子中的 up 和 down 不是介詞，而是副詞（adverb），它們與句中的動詞構成短語動詞（phrasal verb）。

- What time do you usually get up? 你大約甚麼時候起床？
- Let's run up to the top of the mountain. 我們跑上山頂去吧。
- The toddler keeps falling down. 那小孩老是跌跤。
- Property prices keep going down. 房地產價格繼續下跌。
- The scarf hung down to her waist. 那條圍巾垂落至她的腰間。

3.4.3 用法速查表
Speed check

up = to a higher place 向……上	**down** = to a lower place 向……下
(go) up the stairs (行) 上樓梯	(slide) down the slope 正斜坡上 (滑) 下
(walk) up the footpath 在小徑向上 (走)	(float) down the stream (漂流) 而下
(run) up a hill (跑) 上山	(run) down a hill (跑) 落山
(climb) up the tree (爬) 上樹	(climb) down the tree 由樹上 (爬) 下

3.5 across, over, through

across、over 和 through 都是用來表示「從一邊到另一邊」的意思。

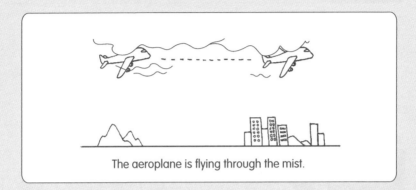

The aeroplane is flying through the mist.

⚡ 3.5.1 怎樣用
Usage

用途

across | 表示從一邊橫過到另一邊，主要涉及平面。

 例
- a bridge across the river
  一條橫跨河流的橋
- An old man is walking slowly across the street.
  一個老人正慢慢走向街的對面。
- The ferry is sailing across the harbour.
  渡輪正在橫渡海港。
- No vehicles can go across the border.
  沒有車輛可以越過邊境。

用途

 over 表示從上面橫過、越過，主要涉及平面。

例
- jump over the fence 跳過籬笆
- The children climbed over the wall into the castle.
  那些孩子翻牆進了城堡。
- They walked over the road to greet me. 他們走過街來招呼我。
- The bus ran over the dog and killed it.
  巴士輾過那狗，壓死了牠。

用途

through 表示從一端「穿過」或「通過」到另外一端，例如穿過洞口、管道等物，主要涉及邊界和有物件覆蓋的地方。

例
- pass through the tunnel 穿過隧道
- go through the forest alone 獨自穿過森林
- The burglar didn't enter through the gate.
  竊賊不是通過閘門進來的。
- Someone is peeping through the keyhole.
  有人透過鎖孔在偷窺。

也表示從兩旁的一群事物或一堆物體中穿過：

- I couldn't see through the mist. 薄霧籠罩，我甚麼也看不見。
- She pushed her way through the crowd to the door.
  她擠過人群，來到門口。

也表示在某地區的範圍內穿過：

- They are cycling through Taichung and Kaohsiung.
  他們正在騎自行車環遊台中和高雄。
- He drove straight through a red traffic light. 他直闖了紅燈。

3.5.2 注意
Notes

1) across 和 over 兩者都表示從一側到另一側的移動，有時沒有明確的劃分，在一些上下文中兩者甚至可以互相替代對方。

> 例
> - He drove across / over the bridge. 他開着汽車過了橋。
> - The ball rolled across / over the grass. 球滾過草地。

如果越過的是一個高的物體，就用 over（如 climb over the wall）。如果穿過的是一個平面，就用 across（如 walk across the street）。

2) across 和 through 的意思雖然相近，不過前者的重點在於「從一邊到另一邊」，而後者則是「從一點到另一點」。實際上，前者「穿過」的大多沒有障礙，感覺上比較容易。相反，後者「穿過」的有或多或少的障礙或阻隔，感覺上比較吃力。

3) 比較位置介詞 across from，另參見 2.8。

3.5.3 用法速查表
Speed check

across = to the other side of 穿過，橫越平面	over = across to the other side 從上面橫過、越過	through = from one end to the other 穿過，通過管道
across the harbour 橫渡海港	over the fence 越過籬笆	through the forest 穿過森林
across a river 橫跨河流	over a river 越過河流	through the tunnel 穿過隧道
run across the street 跑着穿越街道	jump over the ditch 跳過水溝	peep through the keyhole 透過鎖孔偷窺

3.6 along, around, past

along、around 和 past 用來表示不同的移動姿態。

| I am walking along a mountain track. | We are sitting around a campfire. | I have walked past the mail box. |

3.6.1 怎樣用
Usage

用途

 解作順着，例如向着某物的盡頭，如路的盡頭前進。

例
- along a mountain track 沿着一條山間小徑
- along the street 沿着這條街道
- The couple paces along the seashore.
  一對夫婦沿着海邊踱步。
- The drunkard failed to walk along a straight line.
  醉漢不能沿着直線走。

用途

around (也作 round) 解作「圍繞」或「在……附近」。

 例
- dance (a)round the bonfire 圍着營火跳舞
- The students are running (a)round the campus.
  學生圍着校園跑。
- We walked (a)round the town. 我們在城裏到處走走。
- Most staff members have lunch (a)round their workplaces.
  大多數工作人員在他們的工作地點附近吃午飯。

We are sitting around the bonfire.

用途

past 解作「經過」,例如從某人或某物旁邊經過。

 例
- I don't want to walk past the cemetery. 我不想經過墓地。
- An ambulance has just driven past me.
  一輛救護車剛剛在我身旁駛過。
- The murderer was last seen walking past the car park.
  有人見到謀殺犯在停車場走過,那是他最後一次露面。

3.6.2 注意
Notes

1) 方向介詞 along 和 past 的主要分別在於前者後接一個可以遊走的線面，而後者後接一個擦身而過的點。

2) 作為方向介詞時，around 和 round 基本上是可以互換的。在英語口語或美式英語，round 比較 around 常用，但 around 在書面英語，亦頗常見。

3) 不要把介詞 past 和動詞 passed 混淆。

 ✓ I saw Mary go past the post office.
　　　✗ I saw Mary go passed the post office.
　　　我看到瑪莉在郵局前經過。
　　　（比較：Mary passed the post office on her way back home.）

4) past 也是時間介詞，另參見 1.2。

3.6.3 用法速查表
Speed check

around (round) 圍繞，旋轉	along 順着	past 經過
(a)round the bonfire 圍繞營火	along the seashore 順着海邊	past the cemetery 經過墓地
(a)round the campus 圍繞校園	along a straight line 順着直線	past me 經過我
(a)round the workplace 在工作地點附近	along a path 順着路徑	past the post office 經過郵局
(a)round the library 在圖書館附近	along the corridor 順着走廊	past a policeman 經過一個警察

04 PREPOSITIONS FOR AGENT
表示施行者的介詞

在語法學中，施行者或施事者 (agent) 指執行動詞動作的人或物，
表示施行者關係的介詞只有兩個：by 與 with。

The cat is fed by me.

4.1 by

作為一個表達施行者關係的介詞，by 的意思是「被」。

 ### 4.1.1 怎樣用
Usage

用途

 用於被動語態（passive voice）的動詞之後，表示進行某行為或引起某事發生的人或物。

- The blind man was led by the dog across the road.
  狗帶領盲人過馬路。
- The goat was eaten by the python. 山羊被蟒蛇吃掉。
- The sunlight is blocked by the curtains. 陽光被窗簾阻擋。
- The old woman was killed by her angry son.
  那個老婦被她憤怒的兒子殺死。
- Thousands of houses were destroyed by the earthquake.
  數以千計的房屋遭地震摧毀。

指著作、音樂或繪畫作品等由某人所寫或創作。

- This short film was produced by Steven. 這短片由史提芬製作。
- That book that you are holding was written by Shakespeare.
  你手裏拿着的書是莎士比亞的著作。

要強調動作的 recipient（承受者）時使用。

- The traffic lights are controlled by a computer system.
  這些交通燈由電腦系統控制。
- Dangerous tasks are now performed by machines.
  危險的任務現在由機器執行。

➕ **比較中英文**

被動語態的廣泛使用是英文有別於中文的一大特點。英文被動語態的使用範圍極廣，尤其在科技範疇和正式場合裏，被動語態幾乎隨處可見，凡是不必、不願或無從說出施行者等場合，都會用被動語態。

4.1.2 注意
Notes

1) 被動語態往往可以轉為主動語態，句中的施行者必須放回主動句中的主語位置，介詞 by 給刪掉。

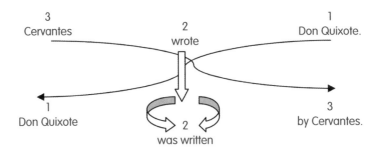

例如把以上一些例子轉成主動句，便是這樣：

- The dog led the blind man across the road.
  狗帶領盲人過馬路。
- The python ate the goat. 蟒蛇吃掉了山羊。
- The curtains blocked the sunlight. 窗簾阻擋了陽光。
- The angry son killed the old woman.
  憤怒的兒子殺害了那名老婦。
- William Shakespeare wrote this book. 莎士比亞寫下這部著作。

2) 在被動語態的結構裏，介詞 by 連接了動作的承受者 (recipient) 和施行者 (agent)。by 後是動作的施行者，比如：Our team is led by Mrs Brown.（我們的團隊由布朗夫人帶領。）被動語態是把動作的承受者，也就是賓語提前做為主語，以起強調的作用。在沒有必要說出施行者的上下文中，by 甚至是多餘的。

- The watch is made in China.（無從說出施行者）
- The picture is put on the wall.（所強調的是動作的承受者）
- French is spoken in Quebec.（施行者非常明確而無需贅述）
- Many houses are destroyed in the earthquake.（動作不是由人或動物發出的）

3) 但有的時候，by 是不可以被省略的，這個時候被動句中必須要有 by：

- People in the world are influenced by Buddhism.

只有是已知或重要的施行者才會在被動句中提及。試讀以下兩組句子。

- The work was completed on time by someone.
  工作被某人按時完成。
- Someone completed the work on time. 有人把工作準時完成。
- Thousands of houses were destroyed. 數以千計的房屋被摧毀。
- Something destroyed thousands of houses.
  有事摧毀了數以千計的房屋。

如果我們不知道是誰把工作完成，在句子中加入 someone（某人）的意義不大。而可以摧毀數以千計房屋的一定是一件很大或十分重要的事情或事件，這個施行者應該在被動句中有所提及。以上句子不是奇怪，便是明顯不足了。

4) by 也是表示工具的介詞，參見 5.2。

4.1.3 用法速查表
Speed check

by
(used to show who or what does something)
被、遭、由

be killed by her son 遭兒子殺害

be destroyed by the earthquake 遭受地震破壞

be eaten by the python 被蟒蛇吃掉

be blocked by the curtains 被窗簾擋住

be produced by Steven 由史提芬製作

be controlled by a computer system 由電腦系統操作

be written by Lu Xun 由魯迅所著

4.2 with

在被動語態句子中,雖然施行者 (agent) 往往是由 by 帶出,形成一個介詞短語 (prepositional phrase) ,但在少數及物動詞句子中,也會用上 with 的。

 4.2.1 怎樣用
Usage

用途

 with 用於被動語態,置於及物動詞後面。

例
- The bath tub is filled with water. 浴缸裝滿了水。
- The slope is covered with snow. 斜坡上覆蓋着雪。
- Little Tom is overcome with fear. 小湯姆恐懼不已。
- Her room is decorated with small paintings.
  她的房間有小畫裝飾。
- During the World Cup the streets were filled with football fans.
  世界盃比賽期間,街上擠滿了球迷。

➕ 比較中英文

切勿濫用「被」來翻譯所有英文被動句的 by 或 with,否則容易犯「歐化句子」的毛病。實際上,中文使用主動句的頻率比被動句高很多,所以將英文被動句轉譯成中文主動句,乃是常見並可取的做法,就如以上例子,如果把 with 對號入座地翻譯成「被」,行文便變得生硬彆扭。

例
- The bath tub is filled with water. 浴缸被水裝滿了。
- The slope is covered with snow. 斜坡被雪覆蓋着。
- Little Tom is overcome with fear. 小湯姆被恐懼壓倒了。
- Her room is decorated with small paintings.
  她的房間被小畫裝飾了。

4.2.2 注意
Notes

仔細研究以上例句，會發現每一個介詞的賓語都不是一個有生命的個體。真正把水桶裝滿的施行者是不是水，而是在句子中沒有提到的一個人。真正把她的房間裝飾好的施行者也是不是小畫本身，而是在句子中沒有直接交代的一個女人。

有鑒於此，with 作為一個表達施行者關係介詞的身份是值得商榷的。相比之下，by 在被動語態句子中作為一個表達施行者關係介詞的角色就明顯得多了。

4.2.3 用法速查表
Speed check

---

with
(used when saying what other people or things are involved)
被

filled with water　裝滿了水

covered with snow　覆蓋着雪

overcome with fear　恐懼不已

decorated with small paintings　有小畫裝飾

---

05 PREPOSITIONS FOR INSTRUMENT
表示工具的介詞

表示工具的介詞有四個：with 、by 、by means of 和 through 。

I am hitting the nail with a hammer.

I am going home by taxi.

I can now obtain the latest news through watching TV.

5.1 with

with 說明完成行為的工具。

 5.1.1 怎樣用
Usage

用途

 with 指用工具做某事。

> 例
> • Cut it with the scissors. 用剪刀剪開它。
> • She opened the walnuts with a hammer. 她用鎚子打開核桃。

除了實在的工具以外，也指用某物或材料做某事：

- She feeds the plants twice a month with fertilizers.
  她一個月為植物施肥兩次。
- Mix the powder with boiling water. 把粉和沸水掺和在一起。
- These photos were all taken with my mobile phone.
  這些照片都是用我手機拍的。
- The carpenter makes all furniture with wood.
  木匠以木材製造所有傢具。

緊接 with 後的也可以是一種手段或比較抽象的概念：

- She won the debate with her eloquence. 她以口才贏了辯論。
- He uttered the name of his beloved wife with his last breath.
  他用最後的一口氣，說出了愛妻的名字。

⊕ 比較中英文

表示工具的介詞 with 多翻譯成「用」、「以」。多看數例：

- You can't catch fish with a broken net.
  你用一張破網捕不了魚。
- The chef seasoned all dishes with chilli sauce.
  大廚以辣椒醬為所有菜餚調味。
- Cats love cleaning their front paws with their tongues.
  貓喜歡用牠們的舌頭清潔前爪。
- He only solves problems with violence.
  他只會以暴力解決問題。

5.1.2 注意
Notes

1) 當被動語態的句子後面不是施行者，而是工具，使用介詞時要特別注意它的意思。比較以下兩句：

- He was hit with a stick.
- He was hit by a stick.

據一般理解，棍子大概不會自己打人。換言之，例句的棍子應該是工具，而不是施行者，所以選用表示工具的介詞 with 可以表達符合預期的意思。

緊隨在被動語態句子之後的 by，很容易被假設為一個表達施行者關係的介詞。句子意思變得有點奇怪，好像是說棍子自己會打人。（另參見 5.2.2）

2) with 的反義介詞是 without。with 包含「用」或「以」之義，without 則指「沒有、無」。

- She couldn't open the walnuts without a hammer.
  沒有錘子，她無法打開核桃。
- I can't catch fish without a net. 沒有網，我無法捕魚。
- The carpenter can't make any furniture without wood.
  沒有木材，木匠無法製造任何傢具。
- The chef couldn't cook without chilli sauce.
  沒有辣椒醬，大廚無法做菜。

3) 不少慣用短語由表示工具的介詞 with 和 without 構成。

- with care　小心
- with interest　有興趣
- with might and main　全力以赴
- with one accord　一致
- with one voice　異口同聲
- with reason　有道理
- without example　沒有先例
- without fear or favour　公平地；公正地
- without limits　無限制
- without precedent　史無前例
- without question　毫無疑問
- without restraint　無拘無束

 ## 5.1.3 用法速查表
Speed check

with = by means of; using something 用、以	without = not having something 沒有、無
with his last breath 用他最後一口氣	without a hammer　沒有錘子
with their tongues 用牠們的舌頭	without a net 沒有網
with violence 以暴力	without wood 沒有木材
with eloquence 以口才	without chili sauce 沒有辣椒醬

5.2 by, through

by 和 through 都有「靠」、和「藉着」的意思。

 ## 5.2.1 怎樣用
Usage

用途

 by 表示用某種方式做某事。

例
- You can always contact me by telephone.
  你可以隨時打電話找我。
- We sometimes communicate with our teachers by email.
  我們有時會用電郵和老師溝通。
- We can now obtain the latest news by various means.
  我們現在可以通過各種途徑獲得最新消息。

用途

by 表示乘搭某種交通工具或用某種運輸途徑。

 例
- by car 坐車
- by ferry 坐渡海小輪
- She comes home by bus. 她坐巴士回家。
- Shall we go by MTR? 我們要坐港鐵去嗎？
- She goes to university by train. 她坐火車上大學。
- How much is it to send this parcel by sea?
  由海路寄送這個包裹要多少錢？

用途

through 也表示用某些方法完成某事。

例
- Cost budgeting has been improved through computer analysis.
  透過電腦分析，成本預算已有改善。
- The elderly can improve memory through activities.
  老人可以透過活動提高記憶力。

這些方法可以是抽象的概念：

例
- Musicians like to show their emotions through music.
  音樂家喜歡藉着音樂表達自己的情緒。
- Problems can often be solved through mediation.
  問題通常可以透過調解來解決。

⊕ **比較中英文**

表示工具的介詞 by 多翻譯成「靠」、「由」、「用」。

例
- I earned some money by delivering newspapers.
  我靠送報紙賺了些錢。

表示工具的介詞 through 多翻譯成「透過」、「通過」、「藉着」。

例
- The woman slowly recovered from her bereavement through faith.
  婦人藉着信仰慢慢從喪親之痛恢復過來。

5.2.2 注意
Notes

1) 在有被動語態的上下文中，by 有時可以用來代替 with。

- The old woman was killed with / by this long knife.
  那名老婦被人用這把長刀殺死。

不過在其他上下文中，by 不能與 with 互換。

- The old woman sharpened her pencil with a small knife.
  那名老婦用一把小刀削平鉛筆。
- I don't like to write with this pen. 我不喜歡用這支鋼筆寫字。

2) 除了在慣用短語或者成語之外，by 和 through 有時可以互換使用。

- We sometimes communicate with our teachers by / through email.
  我們有時會用 / 透過電郵與老師溝通。
- We can now obtain the latest news by / through various means.
  我們現在可以通過 / 透過各種途徑獲得最新消息。

3) by means of 也是表示工具的介詞短語，意思和 by / through 相同，但起強調的作用。

- She passed the examinations by means of hard work.
  她憑着努力，成功通過了考試。

4) 用於乘搭交通工具的工具介詞主要是 by，但如果你選擇步行，介詞是 on，而介詞短語是 on foot。

✓ She goes to university by train.
✗ She goes to university on train.
  她乘坐火車上大學。

✓ She goes to university on foot.
✗ She goes to university by foot.
  她步行上大學。

5) 不少慣用短語是由表示工具的介詞 by 構成的。

 • by accident 意外地
• by chance 偶然地
• by guess 憑猜測
• by hook or by crook 不擇手段
• by itself 自動地
• by leaps and bounds 非常迅速地
• by mistake 錯誤地
• by nature 生性
• by rote 死記硬背
• by turns 輪流地
• by word of mouth 口頭上

 # 5.2.3 用法速查表
Speed check

by = by means of 靠、由、用、通過	through = by means of 透過、藉着
by train 乘坐火車	through activities 透過活動
by sea 由海路	through mediation 透過調解
by email 用電郵	through faith 藉着信心
by various means 通過各種途徑	through music 藉着音樂

06 PREPOSITIONS FOR COMPARISON & CONTRAST
表示比較、對立的介詞

表示比較、對立的介詞包括以下幾類。

I am dressed as a penguin.

Paul doesn't like playing games, unlike me.

His moustache looks odd against his dress.

6.1 as

as 是「如同」的意思，用來比較人、物件、事情等等。

 6.1.1 怎樣用
Usage

用途

 as 引出某物用作比較的另一物，後接名詞或名詞短語。

 例
- He was dressed as a girl. 他穿戴得像個女孩。
- She lives life as a princess. 她過着如同公主的生活。
- I'm going to the fancy dress party as Doraemon.
  我會裝扮成多啦 A 夢的樣子參加化粧舞會。
- The hospital ward is decorated as a hotel room.
  醫院病房裝飾得像酒店房間。

as (adjective) as (something) 是常見的用法，表達「像……一樣」的意思。

- She is not as old as grandma. 她年紀沒有外祖母那樣大。
- He can run as fast as a dog. 他跑得像狗一樣快。
- Tom's girlfriend is as fickle as the weather.
  湯姆的女友像天氣一樣善變。

6.1.2 注意
Notes

1) 可以說 as 是 simile（明喻句）中的 "喻詞"，用來聯繫 "本體"（比方的事物）與 "喻體"（打比方的事物）。

（本體） 　　　　　　　　（喻詞）（喻體）

- He was dressed 　　　　　　　as 　a girl.
- The hospital ward is decorated 　as 　a hotel room.

2) as 擁有多重角色。 比方說，以上使用 as ... as 的例句中，第一個 as 實際上是副詞，第二個 as 才是介詞。原因是在這些例句中的 old、fast 和 fickle 均是形容詞，而不是介詞後面應有的名詞短語或代詞之類。

3) 正因為 as 有多重身份，只要改動以上一些例句，例如在 as 後接子句，as 將不再是一個表示比較、對立的介詞，而是連接詞。

- He was dressed as the film director instructed him to.
  他依照電影導演的吩咐打扮成這樣。
- The hospital ward is decorated as the rich patient wanted.
  醫院病房根據富有病人的願望來裝飾。

4) 值得一提的是，常見短語 as soon as (it is) possible 的兩個 as 都不是介詞，而分別為副詞和連接詞，原因是這兩個 as 後接的是副詞和形容詞，而不是介詞後面應有的名詞短語或代詞之類。

6.1.3 用法速查表
Speed check

action verb **as** something used when comparing things 像、如同	**as** adjective **as** something used when comparing things 像……一樣
dressed as a beggar 像乞丐	as black as a coal 黑如煤炭
decorated as a hotel room 像酒店房間	as fickle as the weather 像天氣一樣善變
live life as a princess 如同公主	as green as grass 像青草一樣綠

6.2 like, unlike

like 和 unlike 是一對反義詞，表示比較與對立的關係。

 ## 6.2.1 怎樣用
Usage

用途

like 常用於明喻句，表達「像」和「如」的意思。

- It's been a hard day's night, and I've been working like a dog. (Beatles)
  這是累死人的一晚，我覺得我今天工作得像狗一樣。(披頭四)

like 與 as 可以互相替換。

- The teen idol was dressed like / as a beggar in the film.
  青少年偶像在電影裏面裝扮得像乞丐。
- The hospital ward is decorated like / as a hotel room.
  醫院病房裝飾得像酒店房間。
- The rich man's daughter lives life like / as a princess.
  富人的女兒過着如同公主的生活。
- Little Tim is playing with his chopsticks like / as a drummer.
  小添玩弄着筷子，如同一個鼓手。

但在以下例句中，as 不能替代 like。

- Like addicts, fans can't stop wanting more collectibles bearing their idols' images.
  像吸毒成癮者一樣，擁躉無法停止想要更多有自己偶像圖像的收藏品。
- Celebrities are human beings, too, like you and me.
  名人也是人，跟你和我一樣。
- Like any other machines, computers don't always work.
  像任何其他機器一樣，電腦不是時刻運作正常的。
- This robot does chores like your domestic helper.
  這個機械人會做家務，就像你的家傭。

與表示比較、對立的介詞 like 意思相反的是 unlike，解作「和……不同」。

- Unlike plant cells, animal cells do not have cell walls.
  與植物細胞不同，動物細胞沒有細胞壁。
- Paul doesn't like TV games, unlike his peers.
  保羅與他的同輩不同，不喜歡電視遊戲。
- Unlike insects, spiders have four pairs of legs.
  與昆蟲不同，蜘蛛有四對腳。
- None of us knows everything, unlike God.
  不像神，我們沒有人知道一切。

⚡ 6.2.2 注意
Notes

1) 不要混淆 unlike 與 dislike。 unlike 主要用作介詞，而 dislike 則主要是一個動詞，解作「不喜歡」。

- Unlike most boys, Bill dislikes ball games.
  與大多數男孩不同，比爾不喜歡球類運動。
- Bill's classmates dislike him, who is unlike them.
  同學不喜歡比爾，因為比爾和他們格格不入。

2) like 是一個頗棘手的英文單詞。它是及物動詞，意思是「喜歡」，例如：I like skiing. (我喜歡滑雪。)，亦是不及物動詞，意思是「想、希望」，例如：Do as you like. (你喜歡怎樣就怎樣。)。 like 也是可數名詞，解作「愛好」，例如：Do you know her likes and dislikes? (你知道她的喜惡嗎？)。時下有社交網站鼓勵用戶給予喜愛的信息 likes，大概也幫助宣傳 like 以前比較少用的可數名詞角色。 like 的另一個身份是感歎詞，用來打開話題或者填補對話中的暫停所帶來的尷尬，沒有具體含義，例如：Like, who knows how to operate this machine? (誰知道如何操作這台機器嗎？) 或 I was, like, really surprised to see her at the party. (我真的很驚訝在派對上見到她。)。

6.2.3 用法速查表
Speed check

is / does **like** something = similar to 像……一樣、如	is / does **unlike** something = different from 和……不同
like you and me 跟你和我一樣	unlike his peers 與他的同輩不同
like any other machines 像任何其他機器一樣	unlike insects 與昆蟲不同
like your domestic helper 像你的家傭	unlike God 不像神

6.3 against

表示比較、對立的介詞 against 用來比較兩種事物。

 6.3.1 **怎樣用**
Usage

用途

against 可對比兩個事物的差異,帶有「對照」或「對比」的意思。

- The buyer is checking the colour of the wall against the sample.
  買方正在對照樣版檢查牆壁的顏色。
- The government often has to weigh the pros against the cons of different proposals.
  政府經常要權衡不同建議的利弊輕重。
- The dark colour of the shirt looks odd against your fair skin.
  對比你白皙的皮膚,深色的襯衫看起來很奇怪。
- She showed off the ten medals she's won at school, against the two I have.
  她炫耀在學校贏得的十個獎牌,把我僅有的兩個比了下去。

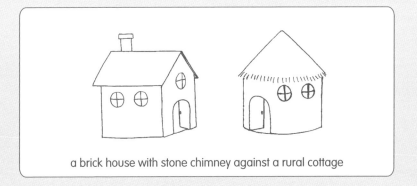

a brick house with stone chimney against a rural cottage

6.3.2 注意
Notes

against 也是位置介詞，另參見 2.9。

 ### 6.3.3 用法速查表
Speed check

---

against
in contrast with; having as a background
對照、對比

---

against the sample　對照樣版

---

to weigh the pros against the cons　權衡利弊輕重

This colour looks good against your skin. 這顏色很襯你的皮膚。

Her red clothes stand out clearly against the snow.
她的紅衣在雪的襯托下顯得份外醒目。

---

07 PREPOSITIONS FOR CONCESSION
表示讓步的介詞

表示讓步的介詞大致可分以下兩類。

7.1 despite, in spite of

despite 及 in spite of 是表示讓步的常用介詞，表達「儘管」的意思。

Despite his age, Grandpa insists on running for an hour every morning.

In spite of the ragged appearance of her Teddy bear, Sis likes it very much.

7.1.1 怎樣用
Usage

despite 或 in spite of 後接名詞或名詞短語，這個名詞（短語）的含意往往跟句中的 main clause（主句）呈現互相對立的關係。

- The government introduced sales tax last April despite public opposition.
  儘管公眾反對，政府去年四月推出銷售稅。
- The fishing boat returned safely in spite of a severe typhoon.
  儘管遇上強颱風，漁船仍然安全歸航。

despite 或 in spite of 用於句首時起強調作用。

 • Despite his age, Grandpa insists on swimming for an hour every morning.
儘管年老，爺爺仍堅持每天早上游泳一個小時。
• In spite of difficulties, many single mothers manage to bring up decent children.
儘管困難，許多單身母親仍然能夠培育出像樣的孩子。

 # 7.1.2 注意
Notes

1) 切勿在 despite 後加 of 或 在 in spite 後漏掉 of。

 ✗ Despite of heavy rain, they went shopping.
✗ In spite heavy rain, they went shopping.
✓ Despite heavy rain, they went shopping.
✓ In spite of heavy rain, they went shopping.
儘管下大雨，他們仍然前往購物。

2) despite / in spite of 多用於正式場合。在一般場合裏，人們多以連接詞 although / though 表達相同意思。比較以下兩句：

 • Despite her illness, the CEO came to the conference.
儘管生病，行政總裁還是來參加了會議。
• Although she was ill, Mary came to school.
瑪莉病了，但還是來上課。

3) despite/ in spite of 為介詞，後接名詞短語；although / though 為連接詞，後接子句。

 ✗ Despite the rain was heavy, they went shopping.
✗ Although heavy rain, they went shopping.
✓ Although the rain was heavy, they went shopping.

7.1.3 用法速查表
Speed check

despite, in spite of = although something is true 儘管（接名詞短語）	although, though = in spite of the fact that something is true 雖然（接子句）
despite public opposition 儘管公眾反對	although the public opposed it 雖然公眾反對
despite his age 儘管年老	although Grandpa is old 雖然爺爺年事已高
in spite of difficulties 儘管困難	though it is difficult 雖然困難
in spite of a severe typhoon 儘管遇上強颱風	though there was a severe typhoon 雖然有強颱風

7.2 for, with

for 及 with 也是用來表達「儘管……仍」的意思。

7.2.1 怎樣用
Usage

用途

for 或 with ▶ 置於句首，後接名詞短語，與餘下的 main clause（主句）產生強烈和意想不到的對比。

- For all her efforts, she didn't succeed.
  她雖然很努力，但是沒有成功。
- For all the nice talk, I don't trust him.
  儘管他說話漂亮，我還是不信任他。
- With all her faults, I still like her.
  儘管她有許多缺點，我仍然喜歡她。
- With all her achievements, she never boasts.
  儘管她成就斐然，可是她從不自誇。
- With all the negative publicity, the company has been around for decades.
  儘管劣評如潮，這家公司卻已經營了好幾十年了。

7.2.2 注意
Notes

1) 使用 for 或 with 作為表示讓步的介詞時，後面的名詞短語常以 all 開始，以特顯其與主句的對立和讓步的幅度。

- For all their efforts, they didn't win the trophy.
  儘管付出了很大努力，他們仍然贏不到冠軍獎杯。
- For all the trouble, the helpers never complained.
  儘管遇上了很多麻煩，義工從來沒有抱怨。
- With all those warning letters, the worker continues to turn up late for work.
  儘管收到那些警告信，那名工人依然繼續上班遲到。
- With all his patience, the supervisor had to fire the late worker.
  儘管有無限忍耐，主管不得不解僱遲到工人。

7.2.3 用法速查表
Speed check

For all noun phrase, ... = in spite of 儘管……仍；雖然……可是	With all noun phrase, ... = in spite of 儘管……仍；雖然……可是
For all the nice talk 儘管說話漂亮	With all the negative publicity 儘管有所有的負面宣傳
For all her weaknesses 儘管她的所有弱點	With all her achievements 儘管有她的成就
For all the efforts 儘管付出所有努力	With all those warning letters 儘管收到所有那些警告信
For all the trouble 儘管有所有的麻煩	With all his patience 儘管有無限忍耐

08 PREPOSITIONS FOR MEMBERSHIP
表示組成部份的介詞

表示組成部份的介詞只有 of 一個。

One of the petals has fallen.

8.1 of

of 解作「……的」或「屬於」，表示與整體有關的一部份。

8.1.1 怎樣用
Usage

用途

 of ▶ 解作「……的」或「屬於」時，置於重點講述的部份後面及整體的前面，並常用在代詞、數詞或名詞之後。

例
- three of her stories 她寫的其中三個故事
- several of my fingers 我的幾隻手指
- the leaves of a tree 樹葉
- the daughter of my teacher 我老師的女兒

事物的部份置於 of 前面，事物的整體則置於後面。

例
- the legs of the table 桌子的腿
- the ceiling of the room 房間的天花板
- This clock tower is the property of our church.
  這座鐘樓屬於我們教會的財產。

表示某事物或某種特性所屬的東西，這種特性可以是抽象概念。

例
- I don't like the smell of the paint. 我不喜歡油漆氣味。
- the importance of the decision 這項決定之所以重要
- the responsibilities of parents 為人父母的責任
- Memories of the past keep haunting her.
  屬於過去的回憶一直困擾着她。

也可用來表示組織或架構中的職稱。

例
- the chairman of the committee 委員會主席
- the head of the marketing department 市場部主管
- the Chief Executive of HKSAR
  香港特別行政區行政長官（香港特首）
- the President of PRC 中華人民共和國主席（國家主席）

⊕ **比較中英文**
使用表示組成部份的介詞 of 時，部份和整體的次序在中英文剛好相反。例如，「房間的天花板」會說成 the ceiling of the room（而不是 the room of the ceiling），而「屬於過去的回憶」會說成 memories of the past（而不是 the past of memories）。

8.1.2 注意
Notes

1) 如果後接 of 的是人物，使用所有格形容詞（possessive adjective）或所有格名詞短語（possessive noun phrase），來表達會更簡單直接。

- What's the name of him?
  > What's his name?
- Who's stolen the car of the professor?
  > Who's stolen the professor's car?

2) 如果後接 of 的不是人或賦予生命的個體，還是選用 of 比較穩妥。

- What's that tower's name?
  > What's the name of that tower?
- Someone's broken the central computer system's security lock.
  > Someone's broken the security lock of the central computer system.

3) 注意動詞的詞形變化由 of 前面的名詞短語決定。

- Memories of the past keep haunting her.
- The memory of the past keeps haunting her.

4) 注意下列兩個短語的不同。

- a drawing of mine　屬於我的一幅畫
- a drawing of me　一幅畫有我肖像的畫

8.1.3 用法速查表
Speed check

---

of
= (shows a part in relation to a whole) belonging to; containing
（表示與整體有關的一部份）屬於……；包含……

the ceiling of the room 房間的天花板

the smell of the paint 油漆氣味

the property of our church 屬於我們教會的財產

memories of the past 屬於過去的回憶

the President of the United States 美國總統

09 PREPOSITIONS FOR CALCULATION
表示計算的介詞

表示計算的介詞大致可分以下六類。

plus, minus, times, by

9.1 plus, minus, times, by

「加、減、乘、除」分別由這四個介詞代表。

 ## 9.1.1 怎樣用
Usage

用途

plus　是「加」或「加上」，提及要增加的內容或數量時，一般置於要被加起的兩個數值之間。

- One plus two equals three.　一加二等於三。
- The buffet costs each of us $198 plus 10% service charge.
  自助餐花費我們每位一百九十八元加百分之十的服務費。

增加的內容可以是抽象概念。

- What you need to succeed is diligence plus some luck.
  要成功，你需要勤奮再加些運氣。
- The internet saves us much time plus physical work.
  互聯網為我們節省了很多時間及體力勞動。

用途

minus 是「減」或「減去」，一般置於要被減去的原先數值之後和要拿掉的數額之前。

- Three minus two equals one. 三減二等於一。
- The selling price minus the cost is the profit.
  售價減去成本就是利潤。

可指漏掉或除去某部份或事物。

- Is anyone going to bid for my DVD player minus the remote control?
  有人會出價競投我沒有遙控器的 DVD 播放機嗎？
- He looks exactly like my dad minus the thick glasses.
  他看來完全像我脫掉厚厚眼鏡的爸爸。

用途

times 是「乘」，一般置於兩個數值之間。

- Two times three equals six. 二乘三等於六。
- Three times six is eighteen. 三乘六是十八。

要表達「乘」的意思，by 亦是另一個可派用場的表示計算的介詞，但它需要與動詞 multiply 連用。

- Multiply two by three and you get six. 二乘三得六。
- Multiply three by six to get eighteen. 三乘六得十八。

用途

by 只要搭配動詞 divide，by 也可以幫助帶出「除」的意思。

- Divide eighteen by six and you get three. 十八除六得三。
- Divide six by three to get two. 六除二得三。

9.1.2 注意
Notes

1) 在正式場合裏，人們多用 plus 讀出 + ，用 is 或 equals 讀出 = 。但在一般場合裏，and 可取代 plus 。

    • Seven and（= plus）eight is fifteen.

2) 以下的上下文裏，and 無法取代 plus 。

    • This new policy concerns you and me. (not you plus me)
   這新政策牽涉你和我。
   • She quickly and accurately solved all the equations. (not quickly plus accurately)
   她迅速準確解答了所有方程式。

3) 減數除了用 minus 表達，還有以下說法：

    • Four from eight leaves / is four.
   • Eight take away four leaves / is four.

4) 注意 times 的拼寫，必須有 -s ，不能寫作 time 。

    ✓ Two times three equals six.
   ✗ Two time three equals six.

5) multiply 和 divide 本身都是動詞，必須與 by 連用來表示計算方式，並不能單獨使用。

    ✗ Two multiply three equals six.
   ✓ Two times three equals six.
   ✓ Multiply two by three and you get six.
   ✗ Eighteen divide six equals three.
   ✓ Divide eighteen by six and you get three.

9.1.3 用法速查表
Speed check

plus	minus	times	by
= +	= -	= X	= ÷
加	減	乘	除
one plus two	three minus two	two times three	divide six by three
一加二	三減二	二乘三	六除二

9.2 by, per

by 與 per 是兩個與計算單位關係密切的介詞。

9.2.1 怎樣用
Usage

用途

> **by** 是「按」或「以……計」的意思。

例
- pay by the hour 按小時支付
- be sold by the pound 按磅數出售

一般置於某計算單位之前。

例
- You can buy them singly or by the dozen.
  你可以單個買，也可以成打買。
- Most office workers are remunerated by the month.
  大多數上班族都是按月支薪的。
- Visitors come through the border by the thousand.
  數以千計的遊客通過邊境前來。

用途

per 是「每」的意思，表示速度或比率。

- per hour 每小時
- per head 每人
- per gallon 每加侖
- 75 miles per hour 每小時 75 英里
- $25 per pound 每磅 25 元

一般也是置於某計算單位之前。

- On average, how much do you spend per day?
  平均而言，你每天花多少錢？
- There are roughly thirty pupils per class.
  每班約有三十個學生。
- How many public holidays are there in Hong Kong per year?
  香港每年有多少公眾假期呢？
- This house is the most expensive per square metre in the world.
  這是世界上按每平方米計算最貴的房子。

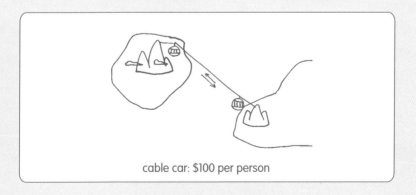

cable car: $100 per person

9.2.2 注意
Notes

1) 表示計算的 by，後面的名詞短語常用 the 開始。

- by the hour
- by the pound
- by the dozen

2) 用 per 表示計算單位的常見詞組，有時以縮寫甚至符號形式出現。

- per annum (= per year); p.a.　　每年
- miles per hour: m.p.h.　　每小時……英里
- per capita (= per head)　　按人頭計算；人均
- per cent: %　　百分之 (= 每百)

9.2.3 用法速查表
Speed check

by (used to show a rate or quantity) 按、以……計	per = for each (數量、價格等) 每
by the hour　按小時 (計算)	per hour　每小時
by the pound　按磅數 (計算)	per pound　每磅
by the day / month / year 按日 / 月 / 年 (計算)	per day / month / year 每天 / 月 / 年
by the metre　按米 (計算)	per square metre　每平方米
by the thousand　數以千計	per class　每班

9.3 by

用作表示計算時，by 還有其他用法和特定含義。

 ### 9.3.1 怎樣用
Usage

用途

 by ### 表示相差之幅度。

例
- an increase by ten per cent 百分之十的增長
- slow by five minutes 慢了五分鐘
- Her father is taller than she by one metre. 她父親比她高一米。
- The ranking of this city as a free society has dropped by five places this year.
  今年這城市作為一個自由社會的排名下跌了五位。

用途

 by ### 也可描述物件尺寸。

例
- one foot by six inches in size 長一英尺、闊六英寸
- a box that is two inches by three inches by five inches
  一個兩英寸乘三英寸乘五英寸的紙板箱
- I've bought a foldable table one metre by one metre.
  我買了一張一米乘一米的摺枱。
- This box measures one metre by one metre by one metre.
  此盒長一米、闊一米、高一米。

9.3.2 注意
Notes

以上兩種 by 表示計算的用法都涉及基數 (cardinal numbers)。

 • by five minutes
• one metre by one metre

 ## 9.3.3 用法速查表
Speed check

by (to the amount or degree) 相差 (之幅度)	**by** (in measurements and numbers) (在量度形狀的) 長、闊、高
by only one per cent 只有百分之一 (的增長)	one metre by one metre 一米乘一米
by five places (下跌了) 五位	one metre by one metre by one metre 長一米、闊一米、高一米
by five minutes (慢了) 五分鐘	two inches by three inches by five inches 兩英寸乘三英寸乘五英寸
by one metre (高) 一米	one foot by six inches 長一英尺、闊六英寸

9.4 from, out of

from 和 out of 表示事物的距離和比例。

 9.4.1 怎樣用
Usage

用途

from 指某人或物的距離有多遠。

 例
- The moon is about 250,000 miles from Earth.
  月球與地球相距約 25 萬英里。
- The bus stop is a long way from the beach.
  巴士站離海灘很遠。
- The temple is fifteen miles from downtown.
  那座廟宇與市中心相距 15 英里。

用途

out of 表示所談論事物的比例。

 例
- Two out of three students in his class wear glasses.
  在他的班上,三個學生之中有兩個戴眼鏡。
- Three out of five users choose this smartphone.
  五個用家之中有三個選中這部智能電話。
- Within this age range, four out of ten were unemployed.
  在這個年齡組別裏,十人之中有四人失業。

9.4.2 注意
Notes

1) from 也是方向介詞，參見 3.1。

2) out of 也是方向介詞，參見 3.2。

9.4.3 用法速查表
Speed check

from = distant in regard to 距離……	out of = from among 從……中
250,000 miles from Earth 相距 25 萬英里	two out of three students 三個學生之中有兩個
a long way from the beach 離海灘很遠	three out of five users 五個用家之中有三個
fifteen miles from downtown 與市中心相距 15 英里	four out of ten 十人中有四人

9.5 for, of

for 和 of 這兩個多用途的介詞也可用作計算。

 9.5.1 怎樣用
Usage

用途

for 表示持續的時間或延續的距離等，具有「達」或「計有」的意思。

- I've been waiting here for two hours.
  我一直在這裏等了兩小時。
- She's going to fast for three days.
  她準備齋戒三天。
- They've been driving for a hundred miles.
  他們已行駛一百公里。
- He sold his old watch for five thousand bucks.
  他以五千塊錢賣掉了自己的舊手錶。

用途

of 可表達「……之中的」的意思。

- He knows only a quarter of the classmates by name.
  他知道只有四分之一同學的名字。
- I need half a pound of cheese. 我需要半磅芝士。
- Dad has brought home five gallons of petrol.
  爸爸帶了五加侖汽油回家。
- Mum has bought us one litre of orange juice.
  媽媽給我們買了一升橙汁。

9.5.2 注意
Notes

1) 以上兩個表示計算的介詞大多涉及基數 (cardinal numbers)。使用 for 時，數值在介詞之後；使用 of 時，數值在介詞之前。

 • for three days
• one litre of orange juice

2) for 也是表示原因的介詞，參見 10.4。

3) of 也是表示組成部份的介詞，參見 8.1。

 ## 9.5.3 用法速查表
Speed check

for (shows length of time or distance etc) 達、計	of (shows a quantity in relation to a whole) ……之中的
for two hours 達兩小時	a quarter of the classmates 四分之一同學
for a hundred miles 達一百公里	half a pound of cheese 半磅芝士
for five thousand bucks 以五千塊錢	five gallons of petrol 五加侖汽油
for three days 達三天	one litre of orange juice 一升橙汁

9.6 below, over

below 和 over 除了是位置介詞之外，也可表示計算。

 9.6.1 怎樣用
Usage

用途

below 表示「在⋯⋯以下」的意思。

- below ten percent 百分之十以下
- below zero degree 零度以下
- a boyfriend who is below five feet tall 不到五尺的男朋友

指某事物低於某數量、速度或水平。

- Most of his colleagues are below thirty.
  他的同事大部份三十歲以下。
- The speed of his car is below fifty miles per hour at all times.
  他的車速在任何時候都低於每小時五十哩。
- The appraisal form shows that his performance has been below average.
  考評表顯示他的表現一直低於平均水平。

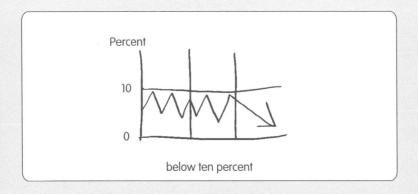

below ten percent

用途

over 是「超過」或「高於」的意思。

- over one hundred books 超過一百本書
- over ten years ago 十多年前
- a girlfriend who is over six feet tall 身高超過六尺的女朋友

指某事物超過某一數量、速度或水平。

- He is the only person in the office who is over thirty.
  他是在辦公室內唯一一個超過三十歲的人。
- Her car always travels over fifty miles per hour.
  她的車速總是超過每小時五十哩。
- The traffic police found her over the speed limit.
  交通警察發現她超速。

A tiger can run over 60 miles per hour.

9.6.2 注意
Notes

1) 有時 above 也可像 over 一樣,是個計算的介詞,在一些慣用短語裏尤其明顯。

 | • above average 高於平均水平 (not over average)
| • above standard 高於標準 (not over standard)

2) below 和 over 也是位置介詞,參見 2.4。

 # 9.6.3 用法速查表
Speed check

below = less than a particular number or amount 在……以下、低於	over = more than or older than 超過、高於
below five feet tall 五尺以下	over six feet tall 高六尺以上
below thirty years old 三十歲以下	over thirty years old 超過三十歲
below fifty miles per hour 低於每小時五十哩	over fifty miles per hour 超過每小時五十哩
below average 低於平均水平	over the speed limit 超過車速限制

10 PREPOSITIONS OF CAUSE AND PURPOSE
表示原因、目的的介詞

表示原因的介詞大致可分以下四類。

I have become muscular owing to working out at the gym from Monday to Saturday.

10.1 because of

because of 是一個短語介詞 (phrasal preposition)，用來表示原因。

 ### 10.1.1 怎樣用
Usage

用途

because of 是「因為」或「由於」，一般置於某些原因之前。

• Parents make lots of sacrifice for their kids because of love.
因為愛，父母為自己的孩子作出很多犧牲。
• He has regained self-confidence because of your encouragement.
因為你的鼓勵，他已經恢復自信。

置於句首時起強調作用。

- Because of his low income, he seldom dines out.
  由於收入低,他很少外出吃飯。
- Because of the poor service, the restaurant has been blacklisted.
  由於服務質素差,餐廳已被列入黑名單。

10.1.2 注意
Notes

1) 雖然 because 和 because of 都解作「因為」或「由於」,但前者後接子句,是一個連接詞,後者則後接名詞短語,是一個介詞。例

✗	He has regained self-confidence because of you encouraged him.
✓	He has regained self-confidence because of your encouragement.
✓	He has regained self-confidence because you encouraged him.

✗	Because of his income is low, he seldom dines out.
✓	Because of his low income, he seldom dines out.
✓	He seldom dines out because his income is low.

2) 留意由於 because 始終是一個連接詞,顧名思義,是用來連接句子中間的組成部份。故此,盡量不要把它置於句子開端。而 because of 是一個介詞,只要後接名詞短語形成介詞短語,便沒有如 because 在句中位置的禁忌。

10.1.3 用法速查表
Speed check

介詞 **because of** = by reason of 因為、由於（接名詞短語）	連接詞 **because** = for the reason that 因為、由於（接子句）
because of love 因為愛	because parents love their kids﹒ 因為父母愛自己的孩子
because of the poor service 由於服務質素差	because the service is poor 由於服務質素差
because of your encouragement 因為你的鼓勵	because you encouraged him 因為你鼓勵他
because of his low income 由於他的收入低	because his income is low 由於他的收入低

10.2 due to, owing to, thanks to

跟 because of 一樣，due to、owing to 和 thanks to 都是短語介詞。

 ### 10.2.1 怎樣用
Usage

用途

due to、owing to 和 thanks to

表示因果關係，一般置於某些原因之前。

- Her absence was due to an accident at home.
  她的缺席是由於家裏發生了意外。
- I missed my flight owing to the traffic hold-up.
  由於交通阻塞，我誤了航班。
- She is slowly recovering thanks to your help.
  多得你的幫助，她慢慢恢復狀態。

置於句首時起強調作用。

- Due to repairs, the swimming pool will be closed next week.
  本游泳池因需要修理，下週暫停開放。
- Owing to her carelessness, she broke her right leg.
  由於粗心大意，她摔斷了右腿。

10.2.2 注意
Notes

1) 雖然大多數外國人都會把 due to、owing to 和 thanks to 三者隨意互換使用，但仍有些人堅持 due to 帶有形容詞性質 (adjectival)，後兩者則帶有副詞性質 (adverbial)，因而限制了彼此在句中可佔用的位置。

- Due to her carelessness, she broke her right leg. →
- Owing to her carelessness, she broke her right leg. OR
- Her broken right leg was due to her carelessness.
- She is slowly recovering due to your help. →
- She is slowly recovering thanks to your help. OR
- Her slow recovery is due to your help.

2) 使用 owing to 和 thanks to 時要注意拼法：是 owing 而不是 owning；是 thanks 而不是 thank。

- Owing to (not Owning to) the accident, she broke her right leg.
- She is slowly recovering thanks to (not thank to) your help.

 ## 10.2.3 用法速查表
Speed check

due to, owing to, thanks to = because of 由於（接名詞短語）		
due to an accident at home 由於在家裏發生的意外	owing to her carelessness 由於她的粗心大意	thanks to your help 多得你的幫助
due to her carelessness 由於她的粗心大意	owing to your help 由於你的幫助	thanks to an accident at home 由於在家裏發生的意外
due to your help 由於你的幫助	owing to an accident at home 由於在家裏發生的意外	thanks to her carelessness 由於她的粗心大意

10.3 from, through, with

from、through 和 with 這三個多用途的介詞也可表示原因。

 10.3.1 **怎樣用**
Usage

用途

from 解作「由於」或「因為」,用來帶出某些原因。

- Sadly, the boy died from the injuries.
  不幸的是,男孩由於受傷而死亡。
- He refused to get out of bed from sheer laziness.
  他純粹因為懶惰而不肯下牀。

置於句首時起強調作用。

- From her attire, we know that she isn't that poor.
  因為她的裝束,我們知道她不是那麼窮。
- From the condition of the packing, one can easily tell the gift has been opened and re-sealed.
  由於包裝的狀況,可以很容易斷定禮物已經被打開過,並重新密封。

From his smile, one can easily tell he likes ice-cream very much.

用途

through 和 with 都是用來帶出某些原因。

- flee their village through fear 因為恐懼而逃離了村莊
- We often sin through our own deliberate fault.
  我們經常因為自己故意的過錯而犯罪。
- The buffet isn't cheap with the service charge.
  由於收取服務費，自助餐並不便宜。
- The cancellation of the autograph session is a true letdown with such high expectations earlier.
  由於之前如此高的期望，取消簽名會真令人失望。

置於句首時起強調作用。

- Through guilt, the murderer turned himself in.
  兇手出於內疚而自首。
- Through hard work, she finished the course ahead of time.
  由於勤力，她提前完成課程。
- With the severe air pollution, international companies think twice before moving to the territory.
  由於空氣污染嚴重，國際企業在遷移到境內之前都會三思。
- With the public exams next week, students are feeling increasingly stressed.
  由於下週有公開考試，學生感到壓力越來越大。

⊕ **比較中英文**

使用表示原因的介詞時，只要後接名詞短語形成介詞短語，它大多數可以置於句子開端或中間。換言之，包含原因的部份可置於句子較後位置。中文傾向於把解釋原因的部份置於句子開端。

10.3.2 注意
Notes

當把解釋原因的部份置於句子開端時，後面需要加逗號連接主要子句，但如果主要子句先行，主句只要不算太長，後接表示原因的介詞前面大多數不用加逗號。

- From her attire, we know that she isn't that poor. OR
- We know that she isn't that poor from her attire.
- Through hard work, she finished the course ahead of time. OR
- She finished the course ahead of time through hard work.
- The buffet isn't cheap with the service charge. OR
- With the service charge, the buffet isn't cheap.

 ## 10.3.3 用法速查表
Speed check

from 由於、因為	through 由於、因為	with 由於、因為
from the condition of the packing 由於包裝的狀況	through guilt 由於內疚	with the severe air pollution 由於嚴重的空氣污染
from the injuries 由於受傷	through hard work 由於勤力	with the service charge 由於收取服務費
from her attire 因為她的裝束	through fear 因為恐懼	with the public exams next week 由於下週有公開考試
from sheer laziness 純粹因為懶惰	through our own deliberate fault 因為我們故意的過錯	with such high expectations earlier 由於之前如此高的期望

10.4 for

表示目的的介詞最主要是 for。

Just for money

⚡ 10.4.1 怎樣用
Usage

用途

 for 表示目的。

- Just for fun 只求開心
- Not for sale 非賣品（不作發售）
- This exit is for emergency only. 此出口僅作緊急用途。
- This reminder is for internal circulation only.
  此項提醒只作內部傳閱之用。
- We raised over $10,000 for charity. 我們募捐到一萬元善款。
- The washrooms in this restaurant are for eat-in customers only.
  這家餐廳的洗手間只供食客使用。

也表達「為了要；為了獲得」的意思。

- She went to the supermarket for some bread.
  她去超級市場購買了一些麵包。
- I am applying for the post of Senior Lecturer.
  我正在申請高級講師的職位。

10.4.2 注意
Notes

1) for 也是連接詞，同樣解作「因為」或「由於」。作為表示目的的介詞時，for 後接名詞短語。如果連接着一個子句，那便是一個連接詞。比較以下例子。

- （介詞）I am applying for the post of Senior Lecturer.
- （連接詞）I am applying for I want to be a senior lecturer.
- （介詞）She went to the supermarket for some bread.
- （連接詞）She went to the supermarket for she needed some bread.

2) for 也是表示計算的介詞，參見 9.5。

10.4.3 用法速查表
Speed check

表示目的的介詞 **for**
(shows purpose) in order to have, get. obtain
供……使用、作……用途；為了要、為得獲得

for the post of Senior Lecturer 為了高級講師的職位	for sale 供賣
for fun 為了好玩	for eat-in customers 只供食客使用
for charity 作慈善用途	for emergency 作緊急用途
for some bread 為了（購買）一些麵包	for internal circulation 作內部傳閱之用

11 | PREPOSITIONS OF MANNER 表示方式的介詞

表示方式的介詞大致可分以下幾類。

11.1 with

我們經常用 with 表達某種做事方式。

 ### 11.1.1 怎樣用
Usage

用途

with 後接人物時，表示「和、同」。

- She often goes to church with her mum.
  她經常和她媽媽去教會。
- Anne enjoys walking hand in hand with her lover.
  安妮喜歡與情人手牽手漫步。
- The two boys are fishing with their dad at the pier.
  兩個男孩與他們的父親在碼頭釣魚。
- Jack hasn't dined out with his wife for months.
  傑克已有幾個月沒和他太太外出吃飯。

My little brother goes to school with my mother.

可表達某人做事時的行為方式。

 • with extraordinary skill 以非凡技能
• someone with previous experience 原先有過這種經驗的人
• She finished her work with great accuracy and speed.
她迅速準確地完成工作。
• He ate with great difficulty. 他吞嚥十分艱難。

I try to work on my assignment with great difficulty.

也可指某種情感或所產生的聲音和動作。

 • with reluctance 不情願地
• with considerable pride 相當自豪地
• with a sigh 歎了口氣
• with a shriek of delight 欣喜地
• She spoke with an American accent. 她說話帶有美國口音。

11.1.2 注意
Notes

1) with 也是表示工具、讓步和原因的介詞，參見 5.1、7.2 和 10.3。

2) 表示方式的 with 和表示工具的 with，最大分別是它們後接甚麼。前者後接人或賦予生命的個體，後者則後接工具、本身沒有生命的東西或較抽象的概念。參見下表。

 ## 11.1.3 用法速查表
Speed check

表示方式的 **with** = in the company of; having 與、和	表示工具的 **with** = by means of; using 用、以
with her husband 與她丈夫一起	with a hammer 用錘子
with her mum 和她媽媽	with a broken net 用一張破網
with great difficulty　十分艱難地	with violence 以暴力
with reluctance 不情願地	with her eloquence 以她的口才

11.2 in

in 的應用範圍十分廣泛，其中一個角色是表示方式。

 ## 11.2.1 怎樣用
Usage

用途

in ▸ 指經歷某種狀態或處境，並受其影響。

例
- in pain 感到痛楚
- in a hurry 匆忙地
- in grave danger 處於嚴重的危險中

狀態可好可壞。

例
- The ceremony finished in good order.
  儀式在良好秩序中結束。
- Passengers are deserted in confusion after the abrupt closure of the train stations.
  火車站突然關閉，把乘客棄於混亂之中。

可以指說話或寫作方式。

例
- The email was in Japanese.
  這封電郵用日語撰寫。
- The patient speaks in a very low voice.
  這病人說話時聲音低沉。

11.2.2 注意
Notes

1) in 也是時間介詞和位置介詞，參見 1.1 和 2.2。

2) 表示方式的 in 和表示時間或位置的 in，最大分別在於它們後接甚麼。前者後接表示「狀態」的內容，後者則後接表示「時間或空間」的內容。參見下表。

 ## 11.2.3 用法速查表
Speed check

表示方式的 **in** (a particular state or situation) 在 (某種狀態或處境) 當中	表示時間、空間的 **in** (a place or a particular length of time) 在某時、在某處
in good order 在良好秩序中	in August 在八月
in confusion 在混亂之中	in half an hour 半個小時後
in a hurry 匆忙地	in the garden 在花園裏
in a shocked voice 驚叫	in China 在中國

11.3 as

as 也是個多用途的介詞，其中一個角色是表示方式。

11.3.1 怎樣用
Usage

用途

as 指某人或物的身份。

- as a teenager / mother 作為年輕人 / 母親
- She is now working as a substitute teacher in our school.
  她目前以代課老師的身份在我們學校教書。
- As an ambassador, the official works hard to promote the city to the world.
  以一個大使的身份，官員努力把城市推介給全世界。

也指被人認為具有的身份或他們的功用。

- as a man of great wisdom 作為一個智者
- be regarded as a hero 被認為是個英雄
- She served as a mediator in many disputes at work.
  她在工作上許多糾紛之中擔當調解員。

My sister works as a receptionist.

11.3.2 注意
Notes

1) as 也是表示比較與對立的介詞，參見 6.1。

2) 作為表示方式的介詞時，as 後接名詞短語。作為連接詞時，as 必須連接子句。

- （介詞） I first experienced the business world as an intern.
  我是以實習生的身份初次涉足商業世界。
- （連接詞） I first experienced the business world as I became an intern. 我當上了實習生，初次涉足商業世界。
- （介詞） As a teacher, our form teacher sets everyone a good example.
  作為一名老師，班主任給我們做了榜樣。
- （連接詞） As we all know, our form teacher sets everyone a good example.
  大家都知道，班主任為我們樹立了榜樣。

另見下表。

 # 11.3.3 用法速查表
Speed check

表示方式的介詞 as 作為、以……的身份	連接詞 as 當……時、隨着、因為、正如……
as an intern 作為一個實習生	as I became an intern 當我成為了一名實習生時
as a mediator 作為調解員	as her job requires 隨着她的工作需要
as an ambassador 以一個大使的身份	as it was an important meeting 因為是一個重要會議
as a teacher 以一個老師的身份	as we all know 正如大家都知道

12 NO PREPOSITIONS 何時不用介詞

表達主要詞類裏兩個字之間的關係時，不可刪除介詞。

介詞是一個連接用的字，用於表達主要詞類裏面兩個字之間的關係，它不可以被刪除。

換句話說，由於介詞置於名詞或代名詞前面，以連接另一個主要詞類的字，使用介詞時，必須確保後面接着的是名詞、代名詞或名詞短語。

若想在一個字前面放一個介詞，必須確保這個字是一個名詞。但是，很多單詞或短語看似一個名詞、代名詞或名詞短語，其實是屬於其他詞類的。

方向介詞 to

here 和 there 經常出現在主要詞類的動詞後面，究竟應否在它們前面用介詞呢？

比方說，我們對以下例子不會有異議，因為置於 to 後面的，不是名詞、代名詞就是名詞短語，它們順理成章成為介詞賓語 (object of preposition)。

- go to London　　　　　前往倫敦
- come to me　　　　　　到我這裏來
- go to the convention　　前往大會
- come to Hong Kong　　來香港

假如我們把 London 改為 there，或將 Hong Kong 改為 here，還應該在前面加介詞嗎？ 答案是：不應該。這一點不是每個英語學習者都注意到的。

- go there　　去那裏　　(not go to there)
- come here　　來這裏　　(not come to here)

here 和 there 在上述例子裏面，都是主要詞類之一的副詞 (adverb)，而不是名詞、代名詞或名詞短語。

對於 home、downtown、uptown、inside、outside、downstairs、upstairs 等字，我們也不用 to：

- Grandma went upstairs.
- Grandpa went home.
- They both went outside.

其中值得一提的是 home，它在這裏是一個副詞，而不是名詞，所以前面無需加 to。這個道理跟 go to church 或 go to school 的說法不一樣，因為 church 和 school 確實是名詞，而不是副詞。

時間介詞

除了顯示位置的副詞，還有顯示時間的副詞和副詞短語，在它們前面也不應該加介詞。

• go there tomorrow	明天去那裏	(not on tomorrow)
• come here today	今天來這裏	(not on today)
• go home this morning	今天上午回家	(not in this morning)
• come back next week	下週再來	(not in next week)

當然不是所有表達時間的短語都是副詞短語，以至它們前面不可以加介詞。

• go there in the near future	在不久的將來去那裏
• come here in the afternoon	下午來這裏
• go home on Monday morning	週一上午回家
• come back in seven days	七天後回來

平行結構中的介詞

平行結構（parallel structure）的基本原則，是用相似的形態表示對等觀念。當兩個字或兩個短語採用平行結構，並需要相同的介詞才組成正確慣用短語 時，這個介詞不必使用兩次：

- You can wear that outfit in summer and ~~in~~ winter.
  這衣服在夏天和冬天都可以穿着。
- The boys were both attracted ~~by~~ and distracted by the girls' dance.
  那些男孩被女孩的舞蹈吸引住了，同時卻又被她們搞得分了心。

然而，當短語的習慣用法需要不同介詞時，我們必須注意不能省略這兩個介詞之中任何一個：

- The children were interested in and disgusted by the movie.
  這些孩子對這部電影又愛又恨。
- It was clear that this player could both contribute to and learn from every game he played.
  這玩家每玩一個遊戲，既能貢獻所有，又能從中得益，這一點是明顯不過的。

不必要的介詞

說英語時，許多人有個不良的習慣，就是在不必要的地方使用介詞。我們也必須特別注意不要在正式的文體，如學術文章裏面使用不必要的介詞。

- She met ~~up with~~ the new coach in the hallway.
  她在走廊碰見新來的教練。
- The book fell off ~~of~~ the desk. 那本書從桌子上掉了下來。
- He threw the book out ~~of~~ the window. 他把書本拋出窗外。
- She wouldn't let the cat inside ~~of~~ the house. [或使用 in]
  她不讓貓進屋。
- Where did they go ~~to~~? 他們去了哪裏？
- Put the lamp in back of the couch. [應使用 behind 才對：
  Put the lamp behind the couch.]
  把燈放在長沙發後面。
- Where is your college ~~at~~? 你的學校在哪裏？

美語的影響

還有一個近年越來越普遍的介詞用法，尤其氾濫於使用美式英語的環境。雖說美式英語頗見大行其道，但仍然有不少人對於這種用法嗤之以鼻，不敢苟同。學習英語的學生不宜刻意模仿。

- The police spokesperson said Friday the suspect had been apprehended.
  警方發言人週五表示疑犯已被捕。
- The latest jobless rate will be released Friday.
  失業率將於週五公佈。

在正式文書上，我們必須補回介詞，即是：

- The police spokesperson said on Friday the suspect had been apprehended.
- The latest jobless rate will be released on Friday.

此外，如果我們在句首交代時間，也必須寫上介詞。

- On Friday, the police spokesperson said the suspect had been apprehended.
  警方發言人週五表示疑犯已被拘捕。
- On Friday, the latest jobless rate will be released.
  最新失業率將於週五公佈。

Section 2: Integrated Sentence Exercises

 綜合句子練習

I. Multiple-choice questions 選擇題

1 The train leaves _____ 8:40 a.m.
   A. about   B. at
   C. in   D. on

2 My birthday is _____ 6th August.
   A. at   B. in
   C. on   D. over

3 Is Miss Lee's birthday _____ August, too?
   A. at   B. in
   C. in   D. over

4 It's five _____ twelve, almost noon.
   A. after   B. before
   C. past   D. to

5 It's ten _____ nine, so we're twenty minutes early for the
   9:30 show.
   A. after   B. before
   C. past   D. to

6 Our art teacher asked us to finish the model _____ noon.
   A. by   B. during
   C. in   D. on

7 My parents sleep early and turn off all the lights _____
   8:30 p.m.

A. before   B. during

C. in   D. past

8 Very few buses operate _____ midnight.

A. after   B. before

C. by   D. on

9 Isaac stood _____ a tree and was hit _____ a
   fallen apple.

A. about, for   B. by, by

C. for, for   D. next, with

10 _____ his age, her grandfather is much stronger
    _____ her father and lives the life _____ a young
    man.

A. At, past, of   B. Despite, than, of

C. For, to, as   D. In spite, than, as

11 The class is represented _____ the Open Day
    _____ our monitor and monitress.

A. for, as   B. for, by

C. on, before   D. on, by

12 Get _____ my way and stop running _____ the
    dining table.

A. in, by   B. into, up

C. out, around   D. out of, round

13   The frog jumped back _____ the pond and then landed
_____ a rock in the middle _____.

A. at, for, of   B. into, onto, X
C. of, on, X   D. under, above, of

14   We had to dig _____ piles of files to locate the one the boss
needed _____ the meeting.

A. across, in   B. inside, before
C. into, at   D. through, for

15   The manager's desk is covered _____ letters
_____ customers asking _____ refund.

A. by, for, for   B. by, to, to
C. with, from, for   D. with, by, X

16   _____ a screwdriver and some nails ready, Father tried to
fix the broken chairs _____ the dining room.

A. As, of   B. By, in
C. For, of   D. With, in

17   Cut _____ the dotted line and you can stick the dress
_____ the girl on the next page so that she looks
_____ a dancer.

A. across, over, at   B. along, onto, like
C. past, by, for   D. through, on, as

18 Employers pay their maids _____ the month and many of
these helpers have to share what they earn _____ their
families back home.
A. by, with   B. during, in
C. for, for   D. in, through

19 _____ birds, bats have no feathers and their wings function
_____ human hands really.
A. Dislike, as   B. Like, as
C. Like, without   D. Unlike, like

20 We know _____ his school uniform which school he attends
and he will be _____ trouble _____ his school
tie, too.
A. by, with, without   B. due to, for, out of
C. from, in, without   D. through, out of, with

II Fill in the blanks 填充題

1 The school is _____ to the supermarket.

2 Don't open the can _____ your bare hands.

3 Joe felt cold and had to sleep _____ a thick blanket.

4 Put the dishes _____ the dining table.

5 Little Jane is hiding _____ the table.

6 Who sits in _____ of you in the music room?

7 Has the government done enough to fight _____ air pollution?

8 Tim acts _____ the spokesman of the band _____ the press.

9 There is no need _____ you to submit the form _____ hand.

10 Some children go _____ school _____ lunchboxes prepared _____ their parents.

11 This jacket is quite a bargain _____ the 30% discount thanks _____ the coupon you came across _____ chance in a magazine.

12 The past couple _____ years _____ an engineering student has drawn a lot of attention _____ her social circles.

13 Refugees sneak _____ other countries _____ asylum _____ the thousand.

14 The delay _____ the delivery was _____ to the adverse weather conditions _____ most of the past week.

15 _____ the time the boy swam _____ the stream, the rabbit had escaped _____ the forest to the other side of the island.

16 _____ an example _____ the entire staff, the director stays _____ his office _____ seven _____ every weekday.

17 Even when his performance has always been _____ average, his company has decided not to renew his contract because _____ the poor economic situation both _____ the city and _____ the world.

18 To get _____ the restricted area _____ getting noticed _____ the security system, one must go _____ stairways full _____ rubbish and _____ complete chaos.

19 _____ his dream, he heard a rocket, _____ nowhere, moving _____ him _____ the speed of light, so fast that he couldn't see it.

20 The little boy made lunch _____ himself _____ the first time _____ his fifth birthday, _____ a little help _____ his mother, who had prepared _____ him everything he would need and cut some ingredients _____ pieces and slices.

Section 3: Integrated Contextual Exercises

 綜合篇章練習

I   Directions 詢問方向

Woman: How do I get to the closest bookstore?

Man: Go straight. 1 _____ the left, there are a few florists. 2 _____ the smallest ones though, you'll find a tall building. Enter 3 _____ the door 4 _____ your right, walk 5 _____ a few steps and you'll see a footbridge. Walk 6 _____ the other end 7 _____ the footbridge and you'll find yourself 8 _____ a huge shopping mall. I don't remember the exact floor of the bookstore, but it is 9 _____ the one selling men's clothes and the one selling furniture. Once you're 10 _____ that floor, you'll surely smell coffee. Facing 11 _____ the café is a long corridor. 12 _____ the end 13 _____ the corridor, turn 14 _____ right and you'll see your bookstore.

Woman: Let me double check with you. Go straight. Should I look 15 _____ left or right for the pharmacies*?

Man: Left, and there are florists, not pharmacies. Let me take you there, honey.

* pharmacies：藥店

II The Director's Speech 董事演講辭

Dear all,

On the last working day 1 _____ the year, let me share with you our year plan for the next. 2 _____ the first month, the Marketing Department will start planning the promotion of our Spring Series. 3 _____ Valentine's Day, when, as usual, all of us will have the afternoon off, there will be a press conference 4 _____ a quarter 5 _____ ten, when the press will be invited to preview our Spring Collection 6 _____ we formally launch it 7 _____ March. The press conference will last 8 _____ ninety minutes as usual and our Catering Team* will start serving tea, coffee and snacks no later 9 _____ a quarter 10 _____ eleven, leaving us all with a relaxing half an hour with the media. A group photo will be taken 11 _____ eleven forty-five and everybody has to leave the building 12 _____ noon. The Sales Department will be the busiest 13 _____ March 14 _____ May, as we tend to make most of our profits 15 _____ the spring. There'll be major meetings 16 _____ Mondays 17 _____ June when different departments will have to draft half-yearly reports to be first circulated 18 _____ departments 19 _____ their respective secretaries and then discussed 20 _____ every Wednesday 21 _____ the seventh month.

* Catering Team：飲食服務承辦小組

The summer months are rather quiet for our company and 22 _____ 2000, we have been organising tours to our branches all 23 _____ the world. With all the seventy-one countries where we operate 24 _____ the world, you only have to work here 25 _____ a dozen 26 _____ years to have travelled 27 _____ the world. The Finance Department will determine which country to visit 28 _____ August. When we return 29 _____ 10th August, after staying there 30 _____ about ten days 31 _____ two weeks, we should all get ready 32 _____ the preparation of the Autumn Collection, our second busiest season 33 _____ the year.

34 _____ the entire September, we'll put on roadshows 35 _____ every other Sunday 36 _____ selected shopping malls together 37 _____ universities. 38 _____ October is another less busy month and the sales won't pick up 39 _____ December when the holiday mood kicks in. 40 _____ the end of the year, there will, of course, be our Annual Ball. Mary, I'm sure you won't forget 41 _____ last week when Paul proposed to you 42 _____ the ball 43_____ the way back 44 _____ your home. Let's see what surprises there will be 45 _____ next December. What I know for sure is that our Christmas Party will be 46 _____ the same date as our corporation celebrates its twentieth birthday.

That's our plan for the year. Susan, how 47 _____ our lunch plan 48 _____ today?

III An Advertisement 廣告一則

Do you have problem 1 _____ the humid and hot weather 2 _____ Hong Kong?

Have you ever walked 3 _____ the back alley where the heat 4 _____ those kitchens and daipaidongs makes you sweat?

Are you tired 5 _____ all the political arguments and the economic recession you hear 6 _____ the radio every day?

If your answers to those questions are YES, then we have excellent news 7 _____ you. Recommended 8 _____ basically everyone who has ever come 9 _____ here 10 _____ an immigrant, the North Pole offers you a cool, quiet and unchanging environment, for the rest of your life.

IV A recipe 食譜

To make Fujian Fried Rice, cut the shrimps you've prepared 1 _____ pieces and marinate* them 2 _____ ten 3 _____ twenty minutes, Heat up two tablespoons 4 _____ olive oil 5 _____ high heat 6 _____ a frying pan. Add 7 _____ minced garlic and cook the mixture 8 _____ a small amount 9 _____ fat 10 _____ diced mushrooms. Put 11 _____ ingredients to make a brown sauce and bring 12 _____ a simmer* 13 _____ less 14 _____ two minutes. Next, add the thickening sauce (a tablespoon 15 _____ corn starch dissolved 16 _____ 400 ml 17 _____ water). Make use 18 _____ a second pan and add beaten eggs along 19 _____ rice. Stir-fry so that the eggs are fully cooked and the grains 20 _____ rice are separated. Add salt if you wish 21 _____ this stage 22 _____ the transfer of the fried rice 23 _____ a bowl 24 _____ which you intend to serve it. Pour the brown sauce 25 _____ rice and serve.

* marinate：醃泡
* simmer：微微滾沸

Section 4: Creative Writing Exercises

 創意寫作：看漫畫，寫故事，想介詞

Exercise 01

Joy turning to sorrow

請按每格的提示文字，以 50 字為限，運用正確介詞寫出故事。

Roy, climb, tree

Rachel, camera, bag, take pictures

turn, hold, two fingers, camera

fall, tree, run away, scared

Exercise 02

The Big Cat

請按每格的提示文字，以 50 字為限，運用正確介詞寫出故事。

tiger, beautiful orange fur, black stripes

hide, the trees, the jungle

creep quietly, prey, pounce

run, 60 miles, hour, chase, some distance

_____

_____

_____

_____

_____

_____

_____

Exercise 03

On My Birthday

請按每格的提示文字，以 50 字為限，運用正確介詞寫出故事。

morning, we, go to, Wonderland, bus

ride the monorail , park

lunch, cafeteria, Underwater World

rent, bike, cycle, beach; leave, sunset

Exercise 04

Telling directions

請按以下地圖地標與路線，以 50 字為限，運用正確介詞寫出方向指示。

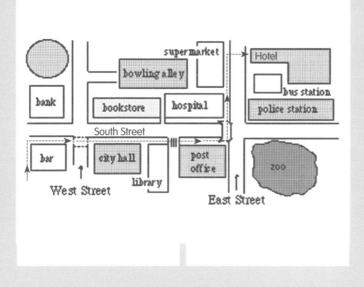

_____

_____

_____

_____

_____

_____

_____

Section 5: Advanced Level

 進階：介詞與其他詞類的組合

✪ 介詞本身是個連接用的字，會與其他詞類組合起來。

首先是有不少介詞短語。它們由介詞和名詞、代名詞或名詞短語組成，當中不乏熟悉的日常慣用短語或成語。

例
- as a result　　　　結果
- in the meantime　　與此同時
- of course　　　　　當然
- under the table　　非法交易

其次，介詞也與置於前面的動詞組合成常見的介詞動詞 (prepositional verb)。由於每個介詞動詞均以介詞結束，而介詞必須後接賓語，因此，所有介詞動詞都一定是及物動詞，後接名詞、代名詞或名詞短語。

例
- decide on (a date)　　　選定（日期）
- leave for (Europe)　　　動身去（歐洲）
- think about (the itinerary)　考慮（行程）
- try for (a scholarship)　　試圖獲得（獎學金）

嚴格來說，介詞動詞跟短語動詞 (phrasal verb) 並不一樣。在語法上，短語動詞由動詞加副詞組成，而介詞動詞則由動詞加介詞組成。 在應用上，短語動詞裏面的副詞，位置較有彈性（如 ask someone out、 back something up、 call something off），而介詞動詞裏面的介詞，總附在動詞正後方。更重要的是，短語動詞跟它本身的動詞，兩者在意思上可以有巨大差異（如 give up = quit (a habit)、 bring up = raise (a child)），但這種情況不會發生在介詞動詞身上。

除了介詞動詞和短語動詞，還有一種結構更複雜的短語介詞動詞。在一般情況下，它是順序由一個動詞、副詞和介詞組成。

- Little Ann looks forward to her first school day.
  小安期待她上學的第一天。
- A phrasal prepositional verb is typically made up of a verb, an adverb and a preposition.
  短語介詞動詞通常由一個動詞、副詞和介詞組成。
- You don't have to put up with his rudeness.
  你沒必要忍受他的無禮。
- The writer has run out of ideas. 該作家江郎才盡。

形容詞加介詞的組合，對英語學習是一種挑戰，因要死記哪些形容詞之後該搭配哪些介詞。錯誤的搭配未必嚴重干擾溝通，但會分散注意力。

• afraid of	害怕
• capable of	能夠
• content with	滿意
• famous for	以……而著名
• fond of	喜歡
• guilty of	犯了……罪
• indifferent to	對……無動於衷
• proud of	引以為傲
• rich in	含豐富的

還有很多搭配會指定介詞的形容詞，需要是動詞的過去分詞 (past participle)。

• accustomed to	習慣
• addicted to	沉迷於
• committed to	承諾
• dedicated to	專注、委身於
• devoted to	致力於
• interested in	對……感興趣
• involved in	參與
• known for	以……而聞名
• opposed to	反對
• scared of	害怕
• terrified of	害怕
• tired of	厭倦
• worried about	擔心

要注意無論是以上哪種形容詞，形容詞加指定介詞的組合，後面都應該是名詞、動名詞 (gerund)、名詞短語或代名詞。

- Joe is afraid of ghosts. 祖怕鬼。
- Who is capable of beating the record holder?
  誰能夠擊敗紀錄保持者？
- Sam is interested in the history of colonism.
  森姆對殖民主義的歷史感興趣。

- Are you scared of me? 你怕我嗎？

否則，以上形容詞後面就不應使用介詞。

例
- Joe is afraid to go alone. 祖害怕一個人去。
- Are you sure they are capable? 你肯定他們有能力嗎？
- Sam is interested to stay. 森姆有意留下。
- Why are you scared? 為甚麼你害怕？

某些名詞後面也會選用特定的介詞。

例
• access to	接近、進入、使用的機會或權利
• appetite for	對⋯⋯有胃口或愛好
• comparison with	比較
• compensation for	補償
• confidence in	對⋯⋯有信心
• demand for	需求
• excuse for	藉口
• faith in	對⋯⋯有信心
• need for	對⋯⋯有需要
• prejudice against	對⋯⋯偏見
• reason for	原因
• solution to	解決方法

同樣，它們都要後接名詞、動名詞 (gerund)、名詞短語或代名詞。

練習答案
Answers

SECTION 2: INTEGRATED SENTENCE EXERCISES 綜合句子練習

I 選擇題

1 B 2 C 3 C 4 D 5 C 6 A 7 A 8 A 9 B 10 B

11 D 12 D 13 B 14 D 15 C 16 D 17 B 18 A 19 D 20 C

II 填充題

1 next

2 with

3 under

4 on

5 under

6 front

7 against

8 as, before

9 for, by

10 to, with, by

11 with, to, by

12 of, as, from

13 into, for, by

14 of, due, for / in

15 By, across, through

16 As, for, in, until / till, X

17 above, of ,in, (a)round

18 past, without, by, through, of, in

19 In, out of, towards, above

20 by, for, on, with, of / from, for, into

SECTION 3: INTEGRATED CONTEXTUAL EXERCISES 綜合篇章練習

I Directions

1 On 2 Between 3 through 4 on 5 up 6 to 7 of

8 inside 9 between 10 on 11 X 12 At 13 of 14 X 15 X

II The Director's Speech

1 of 2 In 3 On 4 at 5 to 6 before 7 in 8 for 9 than 10 past

11 at 12 by 或 at 13 from 14 to 15 in 16 on 17 in 18 among

19 through 20 X 21 in 22 since 23 over 24 around 25 for

26 of 27 X 28 by 或 before 29 on 30 for 31 to 32 for 33 of

34 For 35 on 36 at 37 with 38 X 39 until 40 Towards

41 X 42 after 43 on 44 to 45 X 46 on 47 about 48 for

III An Advertisement

1 with 2 in 3 past 4 from 5 of 6 on 7 for 8 by 9 X 10 as

IV A recipe

1 into 2 for 3 to 4 of 5 on 6 in 7 X 8 in 9 on 10 with

11 in 12 to 13 in 14 than 15 of 16 in 17 of 18 of 19 with 20 of

21 at 22 before 23 onto 24 in OR on 25 over

Section 4: Creative Writing Exercises 創意寫作：看漫畫，寫故事，想介詞

(Suggested Answers)

Ex 1: Roy is climbing up a tree. Rachel takes her camera out of her bag and starts taking pictures of him. Roy turns around and holds up two fingers for the camera. He falls off the tree and Rachel runs away, scared.

Ex 2: The tiger has beautiful orange fur with black stripes. It hides itself well among the trees in the jungle. It creeps quietly towards its prey and pounces on it. It can run as fast as 60 miles per hour. Sometimes it has to chase a prey for some distance.

Ex 3: At half past nine in the morning, we went to Wonderland by bus. We rode the monorail (a)round the park. At noon, we had lunch at a cafeteria near / beside / next to the Underwater World. After lunch, we rented a bike and cycled along the beach. We left the park by / before / at / after sunset.

Ex 4: Go straight down the street. Turn right onto South Street. Pass through the subway. Continue down that street, passing a traffic light along the way until you get to a flyover. Walk over/across the flyover. Walk past the hospital until you get to the supermarket. The hotel is opposite you.